THE QUICKENING

TONY CONTRATTO

The Third Book of
The Agents of Fate Series

Hensley de Vere Press
Lake Havasu City, AZ

ISBN 979-8-9886090-6-3 (Paperback)

Library of Congress Control Number: 2024910000

First paperback and e-book editions August 2024

Cover art by: Nora Hutton
(used under license)

Edited by: Kim Beckham

Printed in the United States of America

Hensley de Vere Press LLC
1799 Kiowa Ave
Suite 111
Lake Havasu City, AZ 86403
hensleydevere.com
contact@hensleydevere.com

Dedication

To old friends...

My college ride-or-die group
Dan, Bobby, Rem, Liz, Teresa, Lala, Walter, Jeremy

The childhood besties
Jay Dub, Matt, Justin, Lil Adam

CONTENTS

Preface

The third entry in **The Agents of Fate Series** was, in many ways, new territory for me. Books One and Two were stories that I had in my head for about a dozen years. Book Three is as new a story for me as it is for you, the reader. It was exciting (and a little daunting) to weave the story together from where we left things in **The Princess of Time**.

Peace in Hayden's world seems to be a fleeting thing. Just when he thinks that he can drop his guard and settle down, new threats seem to emerge. Familiar characters have moments of celebration and moments of hardship. We also meet some new characters that may not be all that they seem.

I particularly enjoyed writing in chapter three from Elle's perspective. Besides Hayden, Elle is one of the characters I feel that I *know* the best. It is always satisfying to me to explore her personal memories and perspective.

Now is a good time to read the short prequel story **The Distant Shadow** if you haven't already. It is available for FREE in e-book format at **agentsoffate.com**

The Quickening

ע

Chapter One

The Quickening of Elle

November 17, 2023

Elle yelled across the expanse of the apartment with a decidedly surprised pitch. "Hayden, come here quick!"

Hayden reacted to her seemingly random yet urgent beckoning. He appeared in the dining room and found Elle eating her breakfast, hardly an urgent matter. His face changed from potential worry to inquisitive wonder when he saw that Elle's expression was one of frantic joy.

"I felt the baby move!" Elle proclaimed, with a beaming smile painted on her face.

Hayden wasn't quite sure if he had ever seen Elle glow with such delight and excitement. She waved her hand furiously, begging him to come kneel next to her chair. Hayden placed his hand on Elle's belly and patiently waited, while she pleaded with the tiny life inside her womb to move again. A minute passed and Hayden felt a faint flutter of activity suddenly springing to life from within Elle's uterus.

"I felt her kick," Hayden said, stunned, as he looked up into Elle's piercing blue eyes. A tear streamed down her cheek.

"I wish that my mother was with us still," Elle said. "She would have been so excited to feel the baby move."

"They know…" Hayden replied. "I'm sure they are watching and are very proud of you."

"Thank you." The smile returned to Elle's face, though more faint than before. She motioned for Hayden to sit and eat.

Dan and Abby walked into the apartment as Hayden was finishing his breakfast. Abby joined Elle in cleaning a handful of dishes in the kitchen.

"I tried asking Abby out to dinner last week, but she kind of deflected," Dan leaned in and whispered to Hayden. "I think I'm going to ask her to be my date for the Thanksgiving get-together. What do you think?"

"I think that if you want to do it, then you should go for it," Hayden replied. "The worst thing that could happen is she says no."

Dan stood up. Hayden's encouragement had served as an invigorating dose of courage. He walked into the kitchen.

"Hey Abby," he started. "This Thanksgiving thing… I was thinking that you and I could go together."

"Together?" she asked.

"Yeah, like as a date," Dan clarified.

Abby hesitated for a few moments before answering. "Dan, I appreciate the invitation, but I think maybe we should just stay friends."

Dan pursed his lips and stood there, unsure of what to say.

"This is really an awful time to bring this up," Abby continued, now directing her attention to Hayden and Elle. "Would it be okay if I brought someone with me? I've actually been seeing someone that I met back in August."

Dan turned and walked back into the dining room toward Hayden.

"I guess that her saying no wasn't actually the worst that could happen," Dan told him and continued his stride out the front door.

Hayden looked over at Abby. "He probably would have preferred it if you had just stabbed him with that knife on the counter. So, since August? Why have we never heard of this guy until now?"

"We've just been keeping it quiet," Abby replied. "He was asking about meeting you all at Thanksgiving, so I told him that I would ask."

"Of course, you can bring him along," Elle told Abby.

"I can't guarantee that it won't be awkward now with Dan being there too," Hayden added as he stood up. "I guess I better go check on him."

Dan looked back as Hayden emerged from the apartment into the front yard. He was sitting in the grass and staring off into the sky at nothing in particular.

"That sucked," Dan said as Hayden took a seat next to him. "I mean, I could live with the whole friends-only thing I suppose, but then finding out that she has been dating someone else was brutal. I've really started to like her as more than a friend in the past couple of months."

"I hear you. I can make you forget it all happened," Hayden joked, hoping that some levity would cheer Dan up. "All I can advise you to do is to go about your life. Maybe things don't work out between her and this guy and she gives you a chance. Maybe you find someone else in the meantime and that's what is meant to be."

"Not to sound like a cliché ass and point out the obvious in an ungratefully semi-jealous tone," Dan

---

interjected. "But you have Elle and that all worked out perfectly."

"Oh yeah, quite perfectly," Hayden replied with sarcasm coating his words. "All it took was her entire family dying, the two of us being hurtled into an abandoned future, and spending a couple of years locked incapacitated in the dreamscape wondering if we would live through it all."

"Hey I did say that disclaimer first," Dan said.

"Naw, I know how you're feeling," Hayden conceded. "In light of the hurt you just got dealt, it's easy to see other things as ideal and gloss over any struggles."

"Yeah, I'm sorry, bro."

"It's fine," Hayden said. "I'll tell you this… I never expected to be with Elle. I've known her for years and we were always friends. We were pretty close because we had some shared interests and obviously because our families hung out a lot when we were younger. But I never thought we would fall in love. It kind of blindsided me. It was all right after Kali turned on everyone and tried to kill me a few times, so I was in a really weird place."

Hayden paused for a moment to collect his thoughts. Dan puffed on a cigarette from a pack that had been sitting untouched in his car for a few months. Hayden reluctantly took one and lit it. They hadn't smoked at all in quite some time. He breathed in a drag of smoke and then continued his impromptu speech.

"All that time in a desolate San Diego brought a lot of clarity. Then the years in the dreamscape just shaped things into what they are now. Three years ago I would have bet against anyone who speculated Elle and I would end up together. Now I can't even picture my life without her as my soon-to-be wife and mother of my child. I guess what I'm trying to say is that you never know what is going to happen. On the bright side, at least Abby didn't try to kill you like Kali did with me."

"Yeah, I guess I should count my blessings. Thanks for the talk, *dad*," Dan joked. "Want to go back inside?"

As the two walked back inside the apartment, Abby and Elle fell silent.

"How's that for an awkward silence?" Hayden remarked.

"Dan, I'm sorry for bringing that up when I did," Abby said. "Can we just forget that happened and move on with the day?"

"Oh yeah, believe me, I will be erasing this entire day from my memory," Dan replied as he slunk into his chair.

"Alright, let's head out and get this Thanksgiving dinner shopping done," Hayden interjected. "There's nothing

------

like wading through hundreds of people at the supermarket to cheer up a crappy mood."

The group ventured outside and piled into Hayden's car. Abby and Dan sat silently in the back seat, unable to shake the tension.

November 23, 2023

Elle stood at the front door, welcoming a large group of guests who had arrived at the same time. Hayden was busy at work in the kitchen, moving back and forth between the stove and a cutting board on the opposite counter.

"Those potatoes smell amazing! Kind of like I'm going to eat the entire dish myself," Dan told Hayden. He had arrived earlier in the day to help with preparations.

"Not if I beat you to it," Hayden joked back. "My grandmother taught me how to make those and they've been a hit with everyone since."

Hayden looked over at the front door as people continued to filter in.

"Clark! Sam!" Hayden shouted as he saw the couple walk inside. He and Dan walked over from the kitchen. "Glad you could make it. We haven't seen you two in a while."

"You must be Elle," Samantha turned and said after finishing a quick embrace with Dan and Hayden.

"Yes," Elle replied and hugged her. "I've heard a lot about both of you."

"Likewise," Samantha said. "We've been out of the loop a little since we moved away, it's great to finally meet you. And girl, that baby bump you have going on is just adorable."

"Thank you," Elle replied, her face now beaming with a smile.

"Is that your new strategy for keeping a girl around, Hayden?" Clark joked and prodded at his side.

"I know, right? Hayden really knows how to…" Dan began joking. His voice faltered and fell silent as Abby and her date walked into the apartment.

"Abby, introduce me to your friends," her date said.

Abby took a few moments to point out Hayden, Elle, Clark, Samantha, and Dan. "Everyone, this is Jared."

A round of handshakes concluded, with Dan opting instead for a brief nod of acknowledgment.

"So, do you go to the same college as Abby and the others?" Samantha asked.

"No, he's a few years older than us," Abby answered.

———

"I'm a real estate broker down in Tustin," Jared added. "Ran into Abby a while back while getting drinks. Saw her across the restaurant and just felt compelled to talk to her and ask for her number. I guess the rest is history."

"Hayden, we should get that stuffing in the oven," Dan said, attempting to escape the welcoming party.

Before they could make an exit back to the kitchen, another group of familiar voices approached. Armond walked up to the door in conversation with Hayden's father and mother, Rick and Annie.

"Elle, my darling girl! How are you?" Annie asked as she came in for a hug.

"I'm good," Elle replied while returning the embrace. "The baby has been kicking a little today. Do you want to feel?"

"Of course I do," Annie replied. "I'm so glad that you're part of the family now."

"Don't mind me," Hayden said sarcastically as he walked up to his mother and hugged her.

"Oh, shush," Annie replied. "Elle is giving me my first grandbaby."

"Pretty sure that she didn't do that all on her own," Dan jested.

"Your brand of humor is always appreciated, Dan," Annie replied as she playfully rolled her eyes. She took Elle by the hand and led her into the front room.

Rick and Armond took a seat in the dining room with Clark, Samantha, Abby, and Jared. As they made small talk, Hayden and Dan returned to the kitchen and resumed the preparations for dinner. Hayden's gaze wandered back and forth between the front room and the kitchen counter while he chopped bits of celery and onion. He smiled as he watched Elle and his mother react to the movements of the baby.

"So, baby shower?" Annie asked Elle.

"Yes, we're having it on the last Friday in February. I doubt the Camarillo house will be ready by then, but it would be nice to have it there if we can," Elle replied.

"How is the house coming along?"

"Really good so far," Elle said. "They are ahead of schedule. The estimate was originally seven months, but now they may finish in five."

"Are you having it rebuilt the same as it was?" Annie asked.

"Not entirely. We made some changes to the layout," Elle told her. "There were definitely things that I liked about the old house, but also I wanted to make some changes so that it wasn't just a constant reminder of the past."

"That's understandable," Annie said. "Are you and Hayden moving there once it's complete? Lots of room to raise lots of babies!"

"Maybe… probably," Elle laughed. "We might stay in the apartment until the end of that school quarter. The baby is due right after finals are over. I'm hoping that she doesn't try to make an early appearance in the middle of one of my tests."

"Well once you get the registry list ready for the baby shower, send it to me first," Annie insisted. "Rick and I want to take care of as much of it as we can. Also, we can help you guys move and get situated in the new house whenever you're ready. Don't be shy, don't be afraid to ask us to help."

"Thank you," Elle replied. "I will definitely keep in touch. Hayden said that he can get everything moved easily, but I would appreciate all the help I can get making the place feel like home."

"Oh yes, my son is probably going to use his little magic tricks to move everything, isn't he?" Annie asked.

"Little magic tricks, mother?" Hayden interjected.

"Eavesdropping, son?" Annie retorted.

"Yes, totally spying on the secret conversation that you guys are having at normal volume twenty feet away from me," Hayden replied as he chuckled. "Still, I hardly count teleportation as the same thing as pulling a rabbit from a hat."

"I'm just teasing," Annie said.

"So, you can actually do all those things that people talk about online?" Jared asked, having stopped his previous conversation mid-sentence at the mention of teleportation.

"I can," Hayden confirmed and then walked into the dining room to provide a demonstration. As he raised his right hand, a portal opened in the room. Hayden stepped inside and it snapped shut behind him. After a few seconds, another portal opened and Hayden stepped out and placed a brochure for the Empire State Building on the table in front of Jared.

"Just like that," Jared stuttered. "You went to New York and back that quickly?"

"He could have just as easily gone to outer space and back," Dan boasted in Hayden's stead.

"Wow," Jared said with shock still evident in his voice. "Think of all the things that you could do with that power."

"Like save the world?" Abby joked.

"And apparently move furniture from Orange County to Ventura County," Annie said, continuing her attempts at humor.

ა ა ა ა ა ა

August 19, 2023 (three months earlier)

Abby eyed an open seat at the bar to move to. The usual group of her, Elle, Hayden, and Dan had just finished eating dinner at Eduardo Quesada's.

"I guess I probably shouldn't have ordered a new drink when we were just finishing our meals," Abby said to the group as the waiter set a fresh cup of vodka and cranberry juice down in front of her.

"We can stay and keep you company," Elle offered.

"No, it's fine," Abby replied. "Go home and relax. I'm just going to finish this up and head home."

"You're sure?" Elle asked.

"I am sure," Abby insisted. "You know I can walk home in like two minutes. It's no big deal."

"Okay," Elle relented as she gave Abby a hug.

Abby settled onto the barstool and sipped on her drink as the last of her friends disappeared behind the front door of the restaurant. She zoned out on the television for a few moments before a commotion behind her drew her attention away from the screen.

"Yeah dude, another one," a man said to his friend as they appeared at the bar beside Abby. "This one was just over a million dollars."

The man paused and looked over at Abby. She returned his gaze, but then quickly looked away and sipped her drink again.

"I'll have a whiskey and soda and my buddy is going to have a margarita," he said to the bartender. "Oh, and let's get this beautiful girl another one of whatever she's drinking."

"Oh, you don't have to," Abby said as she realized the man was talking about her.

"I insist," he said. "I just finished a big deal and want to celebrate. Let me buy you a drink."

"Ummm, okay," Abby gave in. "I'll have another vodka cranberry."

"The name is Jared," he said, continuing the conversation while the bartender poured the drinks. "What's yours?"

"Abby," she replied. "Nice to meet you… and thank you for the drink."

"Don't mention it," he said with an affiliative smile. "Just got a big paycheck and I really don't mind splurging."

"What do you do?" Abby politely asked.

"Real estate," he answered. "I've been killing it lately. What do you do for work?"

"I'm still in school," Abby said. "Computer science major."

"Smart and beautiful," Jared said. "Me, I'm just lucky. Kind of like how I met you tonight... lucky."

"If you're that lucky, you should play the lotto," Abby joked.

"Well, I don't usually gamble," Jared replied. "But I think maybe I will right now. Will you go out to dinner with me tomorrow night?"

"Oh, thank you for the offer," Abby replied meekly. "I appreciate you asking, but I'm not really looking to date right now. I kind of just stick to my friend group and focus on school."

"Okay, I get that," Jared said, then moved a little closer to Abby. "But here's the thing... you're gonna have to make an exception for me, cause I know that it wasn't just a random coincidence that I met you tonight. Maybe we're both lucky."

"I don't know," Abby persisted.

"Tell you what," Jared continued. "You pick the place and the time. Just show up and give me thirty minutes. If you aren't feeling it after that, you can take off. No pressure. I promise."

Abby took a longer sip of her drink and contemplated the offer. She hadn't been out on a date in forever. Perhaps it would be good for her to break out of her normal routine.

"Fine," she finally said through a nervous sigh.

"Tomorrow night at eight. I'll meet you at the pizza place on State College and Chapman."

"Okay, so casual," Jared replied. "I like it."

"Yeah and I can always just take a few slices to go if I feel like leaving," Abby said as she finished her drink and stood up to depart. "I'll see you there."

"I'm sure that won't happen," Jared replied confidently. "See you tomorrow night."

Two minutes later, Abby arrived home and fell into her bed. She held her cell phone in front of her face and pulled up her text messages with Elle.

"I just met a guy…" she typed. After pausing for a moment to think, she deleted the message and closed the app.

"Let's be realistic," Abby thought to herself. "This date probably won't go anywhere. No need to go telling anyone."

The next evening, Abby arrived at the pizza parlor. A quick scan of the room showed Jared already seated. He waved to draw her attention and then rose to meet her.

"Look at that, you actually came," Jared joked.

"I said I would come," Abby replied.

"Yeah, but I've been ghosted before," Jared said. "These days, you never know."

"I can't believe that people do that," Abby said. "I guess I was just raised differently."

———

Thirty minutes later, Abby found that she was actually enjoying her time out with Jared. Their conversation carried on for another hour, in between bites of pizza and the occasional arcade game.

"I had fun," Abby said as they finally prepared to leave. She scribbled her phone number on a piece of paper and handed it to Jared. "I'm free on Wednesday evening if you want to meet up again. You can pick the place. Give me a call."

"I will definitely call you," Jared replied. "Have a good night, Abby."

night, Abby."

⋯ ⋯ ⋯ ⋯ ⋯ ⋯

February 23, 2024

Abby enthusiastically gulped an entire bottle of water down and then picked up a platter of hors d'oeuvres from the kitchen counter before rushing them into the living room.

"Slow down," Elle said as Abby placed the platter down on the table in front of the baby shower guests. "Thank you for hosting, Abby. You don't have to rush, we're all friends and family here. Relax and enjoy the day."

"Okay, I will. Right after I bring out the rest of the food," she replied.

"Let me help you," Annie insisted and followed Abby back into the kitchen.

Elle peered out the sliding glass door to see Hayden and the guys gathered on the back porch, casually puffing on cigars and sipping on bourbon. She could hear the intermittent laughter as one of them would crack a joke.

"This is good day," Abby said as she sat the food down on the table. "Everyone is happy and getting along."

"It is a good day," Elle agreed. "It's been a good few months. No world ending events, no epic battles, nothing but peace and quiet. It's been great, almost like a normal life."

"You better knock on the wood coffee table," Abby joked. "Don't jinx it."

Elle laughed and complied, tapping her fist against the matte black top of the mass-produced coffee table.

"How about you? How are things with you and Jared?" Elle asked Abby.

"Oh, umm, they're going good," Abby replied, not fully expecting the question. "He's always awfully busy with work, but we spend a lot of time together. He's very determined."

"Maybe the next wedding we attend will be yours and Jared's?" Annie playfully asked Abby.

"Oh, I don't know," Abby replied. "It's too early to tell."

"What's it been, about six months now?" Annie asked.

"Yeah, six months," she confirmed. "I haven't really had many serious relationships, so I'm kind of learning as I go and playing it by ear. If it happens, it happens."

"I get it," Elle chimed in. "With Hayden and I, it took several years before we ever even thought about each other romantically."

"Hayden's father and I dated for two years before he asked me to marry him," Annie said. "So, don't mind my teasing, Abby. I just enjoy going to weddings."

"Well, maybe Elle's wedding will inspire Jared," Abby joked back to Annie. "To be honest, Elle, you and Hayden's relationship is like a goal to aspire to. You two are really wonderful together."

"Thanks," Elle said with a smile. "My mother probably would have gave us a hard time for the baby coming before the wedding, but I think she would be happy overall."

"Martha would have been ecstatic," Annie said. "She would have been so proud of you. She *is* so proud of you, Elle. Just as I am. Over the years, your mother used to joke to me about you and Hayden ending up together. Looks like it wasn't just a playful joke, it was intuition."

"She did?" Elle said surprised.

"Yes, indeed," Annie replied. "She never said anything

to the two of you about it because she didn't want to make it all awkward between you, since you were teenagers and our families were always hanging out together."

"That's funny," Elle said. "She was probably right. I would have likely been all embarrassed and it would have been awkward. Looking back though, I think that Hayden and I have been a long time in the making."

"Just think, it all came about because Rick and your father met at that work conference and became buddies," Annie added.

"It's crazy how fate works," Abby interjected.

"We opening presents yet?" Dan asked as the sliding glass door opened and the guys filed inside.

"Let's do it," Abby replied and walked to the gift table to retrieve the first ornately decorated box from the pile.

ينبغي

Chapter Two

Disturbances of Tomorrow

Hayden listened to the faint whoosh of air flowing through the bedroom vent as he lay under the comforter. His eyes focused on the ceiling as the newly chilled air washed over him. He was exhausted, but his mind was attempting to fight sleep. Elle had been asleep for half an hour already, with her head resting on Hayden's shoulder and her arm draped over his chest. The warmth of her body felt like a sharp contrast to the cold air just outside the comforter.

"Just close your eyes and fall asleep," Hayden told himself.

Surprisingly, he found that his command was beginning to work. As Hayden drifted out of consciousness, he found himself waking into an incredibly vivid dream. In the distance, a girl stood at the edge of a cliff overlooking a city. The air was so still around Hayden that he felt he could hardly breathe. However, a hundred yards in front of him the girl's dress whipped about as an updraft off the edge of the cliff rushed all around her. The darkness of the night was contrasted only by the raging fires in the city below that lit her silhouette with dancing red and orange hues.

Hayden cautiously walked toward the girl attempting to remain silent. He surmised that he had failed when the girl turned to face him as he came within fifteen feet of her.

"Did you do all of that?" Hayden asked her as he nodded in the direction of the burning city, gauging whether she was a friend or enemy.

"No," she replied. "I'm here to fix things, not destroy them."

"Who are you?" he asked.

"You'll find out soon enough," she muttered. "Not all those who seem to be friends are so."

The girl opened her hands and held them out at her sides. In one of her palms, she held Hayden's amulet. It shimmered to life, the orange glow steadily rising in intensity until the brilliant light was almost too much to look directly at. In her other palm a wisp of purple energy swirled, quickly becoming just as dazzling as the amulet's glow. The still sky erupted with a flood of black clouds. Their ominous threat of deluge swept through the air with the smell of impending rain.

The orange and purple lights in the girl's palms pulsed brighter. In the background, the cityscape blurred and disappeared. Hayden watched as the emptiness of the bare land changed. The city rose from the dust, returning to its full glory, as if ages were passing in mere moments. The idyllic scene changed again as the city lit ablaze, turning to ash and rubble, and finally vanishing into a lush forest.

"You're controlling time," Hayden concluded. "That had to have been thousands of years in a matter of seconds."

"I'll see you soon," she replied.

The scene flashed into nothingness and Hayden woke up, his heart beating rapidly. He sighed as he briefly pondered the meaning of the dream, but found that the vision had physically exhausted him. He pulled Elle in closer and fell into a mundane slumber.

℘ ℘ ℘ ℘ ℘ ℘

Particles of a muted red sand rose into the air, lingering for a few moments and marking the rare phenomenon of an arrival on the planet Moira. A young man descended from the sky and set foot on the unremarkable landscape of dirt and stone.

"Okay, Amaris, she's somewhere in this star system," the young man said to himself. "I saw this planet in her memories, so let's start here."

Amaris trudged through the bleak expanse for hours. Each plodding step kicking up dust that probably hadn't seen biological contact since the planet's formation. He kept his eyes open for any sign of Kali, any place that her body could be stored away. He found more of the same. There were no caves, no alcoves, no slightly-hidden crevices in the stone. His frustration grew as the hours ticked by, until he concluded that perhaps his mother was not on this planet.

"Let's check the next forsaken rock in this system," he muttered.

An hour later, Amaris touched down on another planet. The frustration seemed to clear from his demeanor as he looked around and noticed the surface was nothing like Moira. His pace quickened as he headed toward the first cave. After another two hours of searching, he came to the entrance of a cave covered with boulders.

"This definitely does not look like a natural occurrence," he said to himself.

Amaris began pulling the stones down, slowly opening a hole large enough for his body to fit through. The

———

rough edges of rock scratched at his torso as he crawled inside. The interior of the cave came into focus as his eyes adjusted to the darkness. The sound of his footsteps broke the still silence as he proceeded down the long passage toward the back of the cavern. As he came closer to the dead-end, the shape of an object on the ground came into view.

"This must be it," Amaris said to himself as he continued on toward the end of the room.

The shimmering object became clear as Amaris stopped in front of it. On the stone floor lay the body of a female, enveloped in a translucent forcefield-like bubble that shimmered faintly amidst the darkness. He knelt down to get a closer look and analyze the scene. Through the wisps of blonde hair partially covering her face, Amaris could tell that this was Kali. Dried blood stained the bottom of her shirt and almost the entirety of her pants. It was obvious that she had been dealt a mortal wound.

"I had to see it for myself and now I have," Amaris' words echoed in the cave. He continued, as if his mother could hear him talking. "Why would he do this to you when he professed to love you? I don't possess the power to save you yet, but I will. I promise you. I will be back for you."

Amaris stood and ran his hands through his hair in frustration. He ran through his plan in his mind as he kept his gaze locked on Kali. "Okay, let's do this," he said aloud as he held his hand out in front of himself. With the flick of his wrist, a bright orange portal opened in front of him and he stepped inside.

ಬ ಬ ಬ ಬ ಬ ಬ

Earth - Chino, California - 2047

Amaris arranged the contents of an abandoned warehouse office that he had decided to make his de facto base of operations. When he had stepped out of the portal, he'd found a bleak reality. It was nothing like the planet he had seen in his mother's memories. He deduced that during his time looking for Kali on the planet Moira, the time dilation pushed him twenty-four years into the future. Some cataclysmic event had long since left the area mostly devoid of human life. The cityscape was covered in a constant brownish-grey cloud cover that permitted little sunlight to reach the surface.

"Now that this place looks more like home, let's head to Fullerton and see if Hayden left any remnants of insight on how he managed to travel backwards in time."

As he portalled into the apartment that had once

belonged to Hayden and Elle, he sifted through the debris and found photos of some other family.

"Great, some time between then and now they must have moved," Amaris said to himself. "Where did you go?"

The hunt for answers led Amaris to Rick and Annie's home in Nevada. Once again, he waded through the dust and debris, looking for clues. After several dead-ends, Amaris found Annie's address book in a kitchen drawer.

"Here we go," he said aloud as he flipped through the pages. "Hayden and Elle… Camarillo. Bingo."

Amaris shoved the address book into his back pocket and opened a portal to the address in Camarillo. Another hour of searching turned up several of Hayden's journals, hidden away on the top shelf of the master bedroom closet. He flipped through the pages incessantly, trying to find answers before the faint hints of sunlight peeking in beneath the clouds faded.

"This won't do," Amaris said. "It took them two years to travel back four? I will have to figure out a way to make that much quicker if I am going to travel back and forth. Hayden used a spell that he must have learned from the Alva'ci. I should be able to refine this, given enough time."

He clasped the journal shut and proceeded back to the warehouse in Chino to work on his newest goal. As he settled into a chair, Amaris sighed at the realization that his mission was not going to be so cut-and-dry or quick as he had hoped for. He pored through the pages once again under candlelight and analyzed the methods Hayden had used.

ℭ ℭ ℭ ℭ ℭ ℭ

Chino, California - 2049

"That's about as good as we're going to get it," Amaris mumbled, both to himself and the young woman chained to the concrete wall. "The math all works out and the changes to the spell look good."

Over the course of two years spent in a sort-of research and development phase for quicker time travel, Amaris had taken to hunting down wandering survivors as entertainment to break up the monotony and loneliness. A typical break from work included tracking a group through the city, killing the males, and taking any females as prisoners. Amaris would use the power of Ane'illuminus to make his prisoners subservient to his needs. Once he grew bored of a particular prisoner, Amaris would kick them out on their own back into the wasteland.

"Time for a test run," Amaris said as he walked up to

the chained female and ran his thumb over her cheek. "Let's get you out of those chains for now."

Amaris removed the cuffs holding the girl's arms above her head and pointed to the ground, instructing her to sit and wait. He disappeared into a nearby door and down a flight of stairs to the basement.

"Time for some of you to go!" Amaris yelled as he approached a caged area in the concrete-encased room. He had built a 400-square-foot makeshift cell from steel bars and chain link fence that he had found in the warehouse and on the nearby grounds. It currently housed five female prisoners that Amaris had captured three weeks prior. He opened the gate and led the prisoners upstairs.

"You four," Amaris said, with his finger pointing out the prisoners he was speaking to. "You are free to go."

The women walked to the exit and disappeared into the outside world. Amaris' control of the power of Ane'illuminus had grown over the course of his quasi-exile in the future. His prisoners were absolutely compliant. He was certain that he could instruct one of them to walk off the edge of a cliff if he wished.

"You and your cousin will stay here," Amaris instructed the girl that had originally been chained to the wall. "I will be gone for about two weeks. There is food and water in that room. Stay alive and don't let anyone in here."

"Yes, sir," the girls replied.

Amaris clenched his fist around the leather grip of his sword as he picked it up from his desk and sheathed it on his hip. His long dark coat concealed it from view.

"To space," Amaris said as he opened a portal and stepped inside.

ↄ ↄ ↄ ↄ ↄ ↄ

Amaris appeared in the dark reaches of space, floating near the planet Moira, just outside the gravitational field of the supermassive black hole. He ran through his plan one last time and then began chanting the words to the Alva'ci spell that he had spent two years laboring over.

"Palkischun Abeva-na-brossney Capseenala. Phohkrano Infimitum."

In the distance a portal opened, flaring with wisps of spectacular violet and pink light. A blinding light surrounded Amaris as he brought up a forcefield around his body. A moment later, his body was pulled into the portal and it snapped shut.

The damp grass softened the blow as Amaris tumbled out the other side of the portal. He felt his limbs and torso and determined that he was whole and without injury. Amaris rose to his feet and looked around.

"This is more like it," he said to himself. A vast expanse of greenery surrounded him. His eyes wandered upward to the buildings lining the streets of Manhattan.

Amaris walked to the edge of Central Park and took in the busy atmosphere of the city. This was the first time in his life that he had seen so many people in one place. He wandered to the edge of the sidewalk and approached a middle-aged man.

"Which way to Broadway and 80th?" he asked.

"Two blocks that way," the man said pointing west. "Cut through Verdi Square and then follow Broadway up for eight blocks."

"Thank you," Amaris replied as he stepped out into the crosswalk.

Thirty minutes later, he slowed his pace and began scanning the storefronts along Broadway. About a half-block up, he stopped and breathed a sigh of victory.

"Breaker Books," he said aloud. "Now the plan really begins."

أن

Chapter Three

Crownings and Vows

March 29, 2024

Elle fiercely gripped Hayden's hand in hers as she groaned through the pain.

"They've been five minutes apart for a couple of hours now," Hayden said as Elle's contraction subsided and her grip relaxed. "It's time to get you down to the hospital."

An hour later, Elle was all set up in a labor and delivery room. Hayden stood at her side and attempted to comfort her through the quickening contractions. He felt a mix of nervousness and anticipation, knowing that soon they would be entering unknown territory in their lives.

"Alright, just a couple more pushes and we should be there, Elle," the doctor said. "You can come on over here

Hayden and watch if you'd like."

Elle nodded in affirmation to Hayden and he stepped over to stand beside the doctor. He watched as Elle continued and the baby descended through the birth canal. A few moments later, the doctor was holding a baby girl in her hands. Hayden stood idly, entranced by the tiny human that Elle had been carrying inside her.

"You want to do the honors?" the doctor asked Hayden while holding out a pair of umbilical clamps.

"Yes, of course," Hayden replied as he snapped out of his trance.

Hayden took the clamps and checked the clock on the wall. After the red-colored second hand made a full revolution, Hayden placed the first clamp. "Scissors," Hayden asked as he held his hand out, placed the second clamp, and then made the cut.

"Here's Kiera," Hayden said to Elle as he laid the baby on her chest.

₧ ₧ ₧ ₧ ₧ ₧

May 4, 2024 - Camarillo

Abby pulled her cell phone from her pocket and glanced

down at the screen. The notifications for twenty-eight text messages and nine missed calls haunted the screen, all from Jared and all within the previous thirty minutes. She slid the phone back into her pocket and refocused her attention on the table full of people in front of her.

"Where were we?" Abby asked the group. Her cell phone vibrated again with another notification.

"I was just about to go to the kitchen and get us all another bottle of wine," Hayden's sister Jillian said.

"Thank you," Elle said. "It's so awesome that you were able to come into town early and be here tonight. It seems like I haven't seen you in forever."

"Yeah, it's great to finally meet you," Abby added.

"You too, Abby," Jillian replied. "Yeah, Eddie and I have been back east for quite a while, but I definitely wasn't going to miss one of my friends getting married to my big brother."

"Crazy, right?" Elle joked.

"So, I know that you two liked this last bottle of wine," Jillian said in reference to Elle and Abby before turning to the other guests in the room. "Amanda, Maddie, are you guys cool with another bottle of pinot grigio?"

"Yeah, I liked it!" Amanda replied and looked over at Maddie who nodded her head in agreement.

"So, the house looks really good, Elle," Amanda said. "I love the little changes that you made. Are you going to be moving back in here fulltime soon?"

"Thank you," Elle replied. "Yeah, we've been going back and forth between here and Fullerton. After the wedding, we will be here all the time. We're keeping the apartment in Fullerton though as kind of a backup place to stay at when needed since it's in a convenient location."

"So we all get to start hanging out again?" Maddie chimed in. "We haven't been able to see you much since the whole meteorite disaster happened and you left for Fullerton."

"Yes, we will definitely see each other more often," Elle confirmed. "I just might get interrupted by diaper changes and bottles sometimes. How has everyone else been since the meteorite disaster?"

"Well, we're still going to classes in portable buildings since the school was destroyed," Amanda said. "The classes are a lot smaller. I think they said on the news that about sixty-five percent of the city's population died. Everyone is trying to act semi-normal. I'm living with my mom and little sister. My dad was out getting the oil changed in his car that day and the place he was at got hit."

"Yeah, and I'm still living with my aunt and uncle," Maddie added. "My parents were both at the grocery store when it was hit."

"I'm glad that both of you are okay," Elle said somberly.

"Okay, let's not ruin the mood," Amanda interrupted. "Let's focus on the positive, enjoy hanging out with each other, and have a good night. This is your bachelorette party, Elle."

"You're right," Elle replied as Jillian returned with a new bottle of wine. "Let's have another glass and play a game!"

The group of girls looked at each other and then over at the front door as a series of quick knocks echoed through the front room.

"Abby, you better not have booked a stripper or something," Elle said with a serious look on her face.

"I didn't! I swear!" Abby replied. Her phone began vibrating in her pocket once again, this time indicating a phone call. She looked at the screen to see that it was Jared and her heart sunk as she realized who was at the door. "Oh my God, Elle can excuse me for a moment, please?"

"Everything okay?" Elle's voice now marked with concern.

"Yeah, it'll be fine," Abby said embarrassed as she marched to answer the door.

The girls watched as Abby opened the door to reveal Jared standing on the porch. She attempted to speak to him in a hushed voice. Her body language conveyed her obvious annoyance at the intrusion to everyone else in the room.

"I tried calling you and texting you," Jared said, not matching Abby's low volume. "I just wanted to make sure you're okay."

"I've been gone a couple hours," Abby replied, her voice now raised. "This is the only place I've been since I left Fullerton. You can even see that, my location is on."

"Well, when you didn't answer I got concerned," Jared said, his speech slightly slurred.

"I'm with the girls," Abby protested. "We're focusing on each other and hanging out. None of them are on their phones. Hell, Elle's phone isn't even in the same room as her. You don't see Hayden over here standing on the front porch, do you?"

"Well, screw me for caring," Jared said indignantly.

"Yeah, I'm sure that's why you stopped by. Just because you care and were worried about my safety," Abby snapped back. "Just go home, Jared. I'll be back in Fullerton tomorrow."

"Fine," Jared quipped before turning and walking back to his car.

As Abby closed the door, the sound of Jared's car engine revving up echoed through the front yard and into the house. She turned back to the group of girls in the living room, her face bright red in a mixture of embarrassment and anger.

"I'm so, so sorry, Elle," Abby said, attempting to hold back tears. "I'm sorry that you all had to see that."

"You okay?" Jillian asked. "Don't be embarrassed for yourself. Be embarrassed for him. That was his fault."

"I'll be fine," Abby said. "I should have just answered his texts. "He gets all over-protective and I should have known."

"What you said… it seems like you didn't believe him," Amanda chimed in.

"It's nothing," Abby said, then paused. "I mean, part of me feels like he was just here to make sure that there were no guys here."

"I've known some guys like that," Jillian said. "You need to stand up for yourself and lay down some boundaries. Just some friendly advice."

"I will," Abby replied and wiped her eyes. "I'm okay. I'm over it. Let's play that game now, please. Forget that ever happened."

Elle motioned to Abby to rejoin the group in the living room. The tension in the air lifted slightly as Elle spread a deck of cards out in a circle on the coffee table and the group began the first round of King's Cup.

Elle found that her nerves were getting the better of her as she lay in bed trying to fall asleep. She knew that it was important that she get plenty of rest before the wedding, but millions of things were running through her mind. She looked over to see Hayden was fast asleep next to her.

"Must be nice," she thought. "Okay, let's try to stop thinking about all the what-if's for tomorrow and concentrate on happy memories. Maybe that will help me sleep."

She rustled around for a few moments and settled her head into the pillow. Once she was comfortable, Elle took a deep breath and recalled past memories with Hayden. Her mind first wandered to the night they met. Her and Hayden's parents had arranged a barbecue dinner party at the Hensley's home. She remembered that music was playing throughout the house and the lights were dimmed. Elle's mother had set out an assortment of hors d'oeuvres on the kitchen table. The french doors leading to the backyard were propped open putting the pool and ornately decorated yard on display.

When Hayden's family arrived, Elle had been in the dining room snacking on cheese cubes that her mother had made her cut up earlier. Rick and Annie entered, followed by Hayden and his younger brother and sister. Rick introduced the kids to everyone. Hayden politely shook hands and said hello to Elle's father, mother, and older brother. When Hayden made his way down the line to her, he made a casual joke about the several cubes of cheese she still had in her hand.

"I still remember what he was wearing that night," Elle recalled. "That black wool coat with the silver buttons."

She had no proof that there was anything there between them at their first meeting. In fact, she was sure that Hayden was just being friendly. However, Elle remembered that her interest had been piqued in the moment.

Elle's memory jumped forward. Her and Hayden's families had become good friends. They saw each other often for dinners, parties, and at events. She thought about the night of her school's winter formal dance in early 2019. Her parents had gone out of town for the night, so she caught a ride with one of her friend's parents. The dance turned out to be a horrible experience, with the guy that asked her out abandoning her for another girl mid-way through the event.

Her friend had made a half-hearted attempt to cheer her up as Elle sat on the floor of the restroom with her back up against the wall, sobbing and sniffling. When her friend had determined that she was missing too much of the dance, she left Elle to fend for herself.

In a moment that Elle wasn't quite sure counted as desperation or inspiration, she called Hayden's cell phone. When he answered, she tried to hide the fact that she had been crying, but he quickly caught on that something was wrong. He arrived outside ten minutes later and Elle ran outside and got into his car.

"What's wrong?" he asked as Elle fastened her seatbelt.

"The dumb guy that asked me to the dance ditched me for some other girl," she admitted. "I heard a bunch of people making comments about it and laughing. Then my friend was no help in cheering me up. It's just been a horrible night. I needed to get out of there."

"Left you for another girl?" Hayden said. "After he asked you there?"

"Yeah," she confirmed. "He had finally asked me to dance after we had been there for an hour already. Then half way through the dance, this other girl walked up and talked to him. Then he stopped dancing and left with her."

"Well, he's an idiot," Hayden told her. "Forget he exists."

"I will," she said as she sighed. "I thought this dance was going to be so fun too. I spent like a week looking for this dress."

"It looks beautiful on you. You look beautiful," Hayden said as he pulled his car over to the curb next to a clearing, put it in park, and opened his door. "Come on. You're going to get your dance in."

"What?" Elle asked surprised. "What do you mean?"

"Get out of the car," Hayden instructed.

She unbuckled her seatbelt and stepped out of the car. Hayden scrolled through his phone for an adequate slow song and then turned the volume on the stereo all the way up as Ed Sheeran's "Perfect" began playing.

"Can I have this dance," Hayden asked as he held his hand out.

She took his hand and Hayden pulled her in as the first verse of the song continued in the background. Elle settled her arms over Hayden's shoulders and they danced amidst the untamed grass. As the song concluded, Elle stood still for a few moments, her cheek still pressed against Hayden's chest. This was much more how she had envisioned her night going. When she finally stepped back, she saw that the pendant on her necklace was reflecting a pattern of moonlight on the ground.

"Look up," Hayden said. "A shooting star. Make a wish."

"Thirty minutes ago, I would have wished that this

night never happened," Elle said. "Now I kind of don't want it to end. Thank you for making it better."

"Well, it's only ten 'o clock," Hayden replied. "Doesn't have to end yet. Let's go over to the coffee shop for a while. We can warm up and get out of this cold."

They departed the impromptu dance floor and Hayden drove to a small coffee shop that was open all night. They settled into a booth and as the conversation flowed, Elle felt her spirits lift. Hayden sipped on his third macchiato of the night and glanced at his watch.

"Midnight already," he remarked.

"Really?" she asked. "I've been having such a good time, I didn't even notice. Do you need to go?"

"No," he replied. "There's no where I need to be more than right here. Plus, with all this coffee, I won't be heading to bed anytime soon."

"Thank you again for tonight, Hayden," Elle said. "You're always so kind to me. Always kind, and understanding, and giving. You treat me so well."

"I treat you how you deserve to be treated," Hayden replied.

By 2:30, Elle was yawning. She didn't particularly want the night to end, but she couldn't deny the fact that she was about to fall asleep in the booth. They finally departed the coffee shop and Hayden dropped her off at home.

Elle's memories then jumped to a weekend at Hayden's apartment, after the meteorite disaster happened and she had moved into his place. The imagery was so vivid that she could almost smell the slices of toast, slathered in butter and boysenberry jam. She had been sitting in the dining room, watching Hayden make breakfast, dressed in a t-shirt that she had stolen from his closet and decided to keep for herself.

Later that night, they had watched a movie. One that Hayden had seen a few times, but she never had. He fell asleep halfway through the movie, finally falling prey to an exhausting day. As the ending credits started to roll, Hayden woke up and looked over at her.

"Wow, I fell asleep," he remarked, his look somewhat consternated. "Lately, I've been almost afraid to just sleep. I feel like as soon as I do, disaster is going to strike. For how powerful everyone says I am, it kind of makes me feel more vulnerable... like a target. But evidently, this felt peaceful enough for me to doze off. Safe, for the moment... You're my best friend, you know that?"

Elle's mind wandered from that memory to the next. She recollected the two years that she and Hayden spent together inside the dreamscape while traveling back in time. At the time, it seemed as though life was nothing more than a series of tragedies. When the shock and pain from one calamity would begin to subside, another one was right there to renew the spiral.

In the wake of the meteorite disaster that had killed her family, Elle and Hayden were abducted from Earth and flung into a dire future. After having spent months in an apocalyptic version of San Diego, they had found a semblance of peace and comfort in their time together searching for a way back.

Elle remembered how anxious she felt when Hayden had actually found a way to travel back to the present. She was confused about her feelings. The thought of finally returning to their friends and family was being thrown off by the uncertainty of whether or not they would make it back in one piece. After all, the method Hayden was going to employ had never been done by a human before. It was a method employed by the Alva'ci race. She felt somewhat guilty about a faint desire to simply remain in San Diego with Hayden. Yes, it was mostly a wasteland. Indeed, it was almost wholly abandoned by humans, save for roaming groups of dangerous raiders. But nevertheless, Elle had become accustomed to it. She had a weird sense of peace and fulfillment in the worst of times, all because she felt safe and cared for in the company of Hayden. Regardless, she knew that it was imperative for them to return to their rightful place in time and put aside her fears.

The first few months of being locked in the dreamscape were an adjustment period. Elle and Hayden learned how to cope and endure what would be their new reality for just over two years. It was unlike anything that Elle had ever experienced before. The simple construct was nothing more than a darkened room containing the duo. They couldn't physically move, but they could communicate with each other. However, it wasn't so much speaking as it was a telepathic type of communication. Hayden made the construct in this way to conserve as much energy as possible. He would need all the energy he could muster to keep the enhanced Chantiatus spell that was protecting their physical bodies intact during the journey.

After they became accustomed to the prolonged time in the dreamscape, they settled their minds in and focused on communicating with each other. Elle knew that the constant conversation was going to be the thing that would keep her sane. They began by recounting memories of the past, sharing childhood stories and dreams. As the stories ran out, they moved on to deeper topics. They shared their hopes, goals, fears, insecurities, and desires with one another. As their journey was nearing its end, Elle felt closer to Hayden than she ever had. She caught herself subconsciously flirting with him at times. Though as she became aware of what she was doing, she observed that Hayden wasn't just brushing it off. On the contrary, he seemed to be returning the sentiment. Elle continued to flirt with him, now knowingly, but still as inconspicuous as possible. After all, they could basically read each other's thoughts. She didn't want to give it away that she felt like she was starting to fall for him. Maybe he already knew. Perhaps he felt the same way… but this was too vulnerable a position to be in, locked inside the dreamscape, to broach the topic and possibly be wrong about it. The embarrassment would be akin to having a nightmare that you couldn't wake from. She decided to wait until they had arrived back to the present to even bring it up. A time when they could actually speak and interact normally.

Finally, Elle recalled the moments just before the portal opened in the present. She had come to enjoy the playful flirtation, mingled alongside the intense personal and philosophical conversations they shared. It was almost as though they had their own language between them, an esoteric spirit where the lines between their individuality blurred. She savored the intimacy that now existed between their minds, dare she say, even between their souls. She found herself pining to be physically close to Hayden in the same way. She worked up the courage to overcome her fear of embarrassment and decided to test the waters on sharing her feelings. If he did feel the same, she wanted to plunge back into the present with a clear direction for their relationship. Still slightly nervous, she brought up the subject by asking if Hayden recalled a moment back in the year 2020 when he had visited her home. Elle was a little perplexed that Hayden seemed to have no memory of the visit whatsoever. However, she carried on and tried to refresh his memory. She was about to pass the point of no return and utter the three words that would leave her exposed and vulnerable. She only managed to say "I…" before the portal opened and spit their bodies out into the present time several hundred feet above the open ocean.

"That figures. Such great timing," she'd thought to herself as they awoke and plummeted toward the water.

The next several hours were all a blur. She and Hayden were caught in a nonstop flurry of excitement and confusion. They had been declared missing after being gone so long, so their friends were full of questions. Elle found that amongst all the commotion there wasn't a good opportunity for her to raise the issue of her and Hayden's relationship again. She waited patiently for the opportune moment. "Well, patiently is a bit of a euphemism," Elle thought to herself.

Throughout the course of the day, Elle's uncertainty about Hayden feeling the same way that she did, began to vanish. Now that they were out of the dreamscape and could physically walk, talk, and interact with each other, it was becoming apparent to her that he shared her feelings. Amidst the constant barrage of questions and explaining to everyone what had happened, she saw the signs… Hayden's gazes during conversation relayed his emotions. It was like pieces of a puzzle falling into place in front of her; the way he talked about her, the subtle touch of a hand, the enigmatic statements hearkening back to an inside joke between the two of them. The evening came, and with it, an end to the whirlwind of reunions with their friends. A new resolute attitude had also formed in Elle's mind.

Elle took a shower as she waited for Hayden to arrive home from Dan's. After they shared a quick snack, she felt that the moment had finally arrived. She was ready. She was determined to make her feelings unmistakably clear. Hayden had gone down to the bedroom to check a text message on his phone. Instead of waiting for him to come back to the living room, Elle followed a short distance behind him. She arrived in the doorway just as he was sending a reply text. She heard him say who it was that had texted him, but she wasn't listening to anything other than the voice in her head.

With every step she had taken down the hallway, her nerves sharpened. Her mind was awash with a cacophony of thoughts, desires, and plans. She could feel her body getting hotter, her skin almost feeling like it was on fire. She wondered if her face was flushed. Would she give her intentions away through a barrage of autonomic cues? As she stepped forward into the bedroom, Elle was aware of each and every breath she took. Her senses were heightened, her body tingling in anticipation. She could tell that Hayden was still talking to her, as she could see his lips moving. However, she had no idea what he was saying. Her focus was on her next move as she now stood in front of him.

"Elle..?" Hayden said in shock.

She had just kissed him. He had been talking about something, and she had just kissed him. She had done it... she'd finally carried out her plan and relayed her feelings. Though she was now paying attention to Hayden's words, she didn't bother to respond. Instead she held his gaze and continued in her plan to make an irrevocable statement about where she wanted their relationship to go. As she lifted her shirt over her head, Elle felt the rush of nervous excitement return. The acceleration in her heartbeat provided her with the fortitude to proceed in her planned spontaneity. She was still looking directly at Hayden as she slid her pajama shorts down over her hips and let them fall to the floor. Here she was… exposed, vulnerable, in absolutely uncharted territory. Yet, she felt safe. Nervous, but paradoxically relaxed. The look on Hayden's face told her that her intended message had been received, deafeningly loud and unquestionably clear.

Elle snapped back into the present moment as she felt her eyelids growing heavier and a cloud of drowsiness beginning to overcome her senses. She laid still in the silence, listening to Hayden's breathing as he slept. The darkness of the bedroom contrasted with the warmth of the comforter enveloping her body. As she recapped her memories, Elle could see the pattern, the line of progression, almost like an invisible thread pulling her along to this point in life. A point of happiness and contentment.

"I love you," she whispered to Hayden just before falling asleep.

 લ લ લ લ લ લ

Hayden rustled out of bed at 6:00 a.m. and gently shook Elle's shoulder to wake her. When he returned from the bathroom, Elle had found her way out of bed and thrown some clothes on. The echo of knocking on the front door reverberated down the hallway, indicating that Abby had arrived. The formality was more of a courtesy knock, as she let herself in and proceeded down the hall to make sure that Elle was ready to go.

"Come on, girl," Abby teased. "Wake up, we have a big day ahead of us."

"I'm awake," Elle replied, still groggy.

"I've got your dress and everything we could possibly need in my car," Abby said.

"Okay, just let me brush my teeth and grab my bag," Elle said as she walked into the bathroom.

"Wakey, wakey!" Dan's voice called out as he stepped through the front door. Hayden walked out to meet him.

"Morning," Hayden said while yawning.

"Coffee?" Dan offered.

"Yes, please," Hayden said.

Dan fired up the coffee machine and the aroma filled the room. Hayden slumped in a dining room chair and attempted to complete waking up.

"Good morning, girls," Dan said as Elle and Abby walked into the room.

After repeating the greeting in unison, the girls made a beeline for the front door so they could get on the road. "Sorry, gotta get going," Abby said.

"See you two later," Hayden said.

Elle stopped abruptly before exiting, turned around, and walked back over to Hayden. "I love you," she said after giving him a kiss.

"Love you too," he replied. "Remember to eat something and drink some water. I don't need you passing out at the altar. Oh, and my Mom texted a few minutes ago. Kiera slept well and they'll be heading to the venue early still."

"Don't worry, I'll make sure she's hydrated," Abby said as she peeked her head back in the door. "Let's go Elle!"

Dan walked over to the table and set Hayden's coffee cup in front of him before sitting down in his own chair. "So, you gonna go through with it?"

"Yes, still going through with it," Hayden said through raspy laughter. "You almost made me choke on my coffee."

"Okay, good," Dan replied. "I'm liking how I look in my suit so it would be a bummer if you bailed and I didn't get to wear it today."

"Well, if all else fails, you could always just wear it down to the grocery store," Hayden joked back.

"True, just stroll around town all dressed up," Dan said. "Plus, I have your and Elle's rings, so I could go trade those at the pawn shop for a new phone or something."

"A new phone?" Hayden mocked. "You're getting ripped off if all you get is a phone for those rings."

"Good to know," Dan replied mischievously while he caricatured rubbing his palms together as if plotting something. "On a serious note though, Armond just texted me and said that he's on his way over with Clark and your brother."

"Ugh, I guess that means I should hop in the shower before they get here," Hayden said after he downed the remaining coffee from his cup.

"Yes, normally people shower for things such as this," Dan said.

"Alright, let them in and try to keep them entertained," Hayden instructed as he stood and began walking toward the hallway.

"This wasn't mentioned in the pamphlet you gave me about being the best man," Dan yelled jokingly as Hayden disappeared from sight.

☙ ☙ ☙ ☙ ☙ ☙

Hayden stood at the altar. The mild sunlight washed the venue with just enough warmth to be comfortable. Hayden could feel the tightness of his vest and suit jacket against his chest as he took a deep breath in. Looking over his shoulder, Hayden saw Dan, his brother Eddie, Clark, and

Armond standing neatly at attention. In front of him stood Jillian, Abby, Amanda, and Maddie. Hayden turned his gaze across the terrace, sweeping the faces of the hundred or so people that showed up for the wedding. They all waited in anticipation.

A hush fell over the crowd as the large wooden double-doors to the palatial main house opened. The crack of the old hinges pierced the silence. Hayden's father appeared in the doorway where he stood for a brief moment before turning and holding his hand out. A collective gasp echoed in the room as Elle's hand took Rick's and she stepped into view.

The crowd rose to their feet as the instrumentals of Canon in D Major swelled. Hayden felt a tear run down his cheek as his eyes met Elle's. Her smile radiated throughout the room. Hayden's father, who was standing in for Elle's father, walked in step with her down the aisle. The sunlight shimmered off the jewel-encrusted bodice of Elle's dress.

"Who gives this young woman to be married to this man today?" the officiant asked as Elle and Rick arrived at the altar.

"On behalf of Gabe and Martha Hensley, it is my honor to do so," Rick replied.

Elle gave Rick a hug and then took her place opposite Hayden. The officiant began with opening remarks.

His words all seemed a blur to Hayden as he stared into Elle's eyes. He snapped back into reality when he was prompted to give his vows.

"Elle, mon cœur… l'amour de ma vie," Hayden began. "I cannot help but feel that it was a matter of destiny that my father met yours all those years ago… and that moment led to you and I coming into each other's lives. I have known you as a friend, a confidant, a partner, a lover, and as the mother of our child. Today, I am overwhelmed with joy to add *wife* to that list. I promise that I will cherish you. I will stand against the darkness of this world if it tries to harm you. I will live for you and I would die for you. Every fiber of my being, I give to you. I will praise you, lift you up, push you to reach your goals, and be your refuge when you are weary. I promise you my love and support from this breath until my very last."

"Hayden," Elle said through now freely flowing tears. "You have been there for me through the ordinary and the unheard of. From day trips to the bookstore and beach, to rescuing me from burning buildings. You are my safety, my comfort, my personification of what the word love means. You give me strength, hope, and confidence. My life changed on the day we met. I may not have known it back then, but I can see it clearly now. Each time you hold me in your arms, I can feel it… that place is where I was meant to be. I promise to give you everything that I have in me. My love, my patience, my support, and my solace. I am yours. I always have been and I will always be, 'til the end of time."

For a few moments, the silence of the crowd was interrupted only by the sound of dozens of people sniffling in an attempt to hold back tears. The officiant finally chimed in and led Hayden and Elle into the exchange of their wedding rings before announcing them as husband and wife. Elle pulled Hayden closer to her and leaned in for a kiss as the crowd rose to their feet and cheered.

ଓ ଓ ଓ ଓ ଓ ଓ

The reception amphitheater hummed with chatter as the guests waited for the wedding party to arrive. The massive structure sat adjacent to the mansion used for the wedding ceremony. It boasted a thirty-foot high ceiling, an elaborate sound system, and was exquisitely decorated. Rick pointed out to Annie the enormous assortment of stage lightning and pyrotechnic equipment scattered throughout the area.

"Oh, I see it all," Annie remarked. "I'm afraid our son's penchant for theatrics is about to come to life in some grand spectacle."

As the lights in the amphitheater dimmed, the

bridesmaids and groomsmen walked in accompanied by a seven-piece band. After they took their seats, the lighting continued to dim until the room was enveloped in complete darkness. A large screen along the wall flickered to life with black and white videos and images of Hayden and Elle. The audio soundtrack was filled with clips of news broadcasts and commentary about Hayden and his exploits with the agents of fate.

"What is he up to?" Annie said aloud.

"I know what he's about to do," Samantha, who was seated at the same table, said in reply. "The style of this video is strikingly familiar. It's about to get really loud in here."

The video screen went black and the room was plunged back into darkness. Intense red fill lights flooded the room and revealed Hayden and Elle, now standing just inside the amphitheater doors. The red light disappeared and was replaced by a white spotlight on the couple. Pounding bass notes boomed from the sound system, supplemented by spurts of fire from the pyrotechnic pillars. As Elle and Hayden walked toward the head table, the speakers blared Taylor Swift's song "...Ready For It?" as the opening anthem for the event.

"Was that everything you hoped it would be?" Elle asked Hayden after they finally took their seats. "People look appropriately surprised."

"Yes, it was worth it," Hayden said with a grin.

"Welcome, everyone," Dan said into the microphone. "As you may have noticed, a wedding reception that features Hayden as the groom is going to be anything but normal. On behalf of the bride and groom, I invite you to enjoy the next few hours… eat, drink, indulge, mingle, and be merry."

The band kicked in immediately after Dan took his seat with a lively rendition of "Everywhere, Everything" by Noah Kahan followed by Hozier's "Work Song."

Dan looked down the table to notice that Abby was still absent. He had assumed that she snuck away to the bathroom during the first song, but he was now fighting the urge to wonder if she was okay. After a brief internal debate, he stood and walked over to the side of the amphitheater to the long hallway that led to the restrooms.

"Dammit, Abby, you better be sick or something," Dan mumbled to himself as he walked down the hall.

As he arrived at the door of the women's restroom, Dan could hear muffled voices from the other side. He could tell that one of them was a man's voice and the other was definitely Abby. Her voice was shaky and almost fearful.

"Abby, are you in there?" Dan called out in a raised voice through the door. "You alright?"

"Oh, great. See what you did now?" the male voice inside the restroom said after a moment of silence.

Dan sighed and pushed the door to the women's restroom open. The scene immediately caused him concern. Abby's back was pressed up against the tile wall. It was obvious from the flush of her face that she had been crying. In front of her stood Jared. His palm pressed against the wall next to Abby's head, in a menacing stance. It was clear they had been arguing.

Jared looked over at the open door to see Dan and then returned his gaze to Abby. "Forget it, do what you want."

"Jared, just relax and enjoy the day," Abby said, attempting to console him about some issue that was still a mystery to Dan.

"Out of my way, Dan," Jared barked as he walked away from Abby and exited the restroom.

"Whatever, dude," Dan quipped back as Jared stormed off down the hallway.

"What the hell was all that?" Dan asked Abby as he stepped into the restroom.

"It was nothing Dan," Abby replied. "Just some stupid little argument about nothing. Too much wine. Everything is okay, it'll blow over by the morning."

"Are you sure?" Dan pried. "If he's treating you…"

"It's okay, Dan," Abby interrupted. "I swear."

"Alright," Dan relented.

Abby stepped up to the mirror and wiped her eyes before touching up her makeup. Dan watched her intently for any signs that might reveal what was going on inside her head.

"Thanks for checking on me," Abby finally said as she finished her makeup. "Thank you for being concerned about me. I do appreciate it."

"You're welcome," Dan replied. "Ready to get back in there?"

Abby nodded and the duo returned to their places in the amphitheater. Dan scanned the room and noted that Jared was nowhere to be seen. "Jerk must have left. Good riddance," he thought to himself.

As the afternoon waned on into the evening, the reception drew near its end. Hayden walked over to the stage and sat down on the piano bench, where he concluded the event with a heartfelt song.

تكون

Chapter Four

Amaris

"Good morning!" Ahsan called out across the expanse of the bookstore that he owned with his brother Armond.

"And to you," the familiar figure shouted back.

The patron, a tall and fit young man with dark brown hair, approached the counter where Ahsan was removing paperback books from a box to sort through and get ready for display. The two men shook hands and Ahsan stepped out from behind the counter.

"I haven't seen you for a few days, Amaris," Ahsan said with a hint of inquisitiveness in his voice.

"I had to go out of town for some business," Amaris replied. "It was last minute. Unfortunately, I have another trip coming up tomorrow."

"Of course. I hope it all went well, my friend," Ahsan said.

"Quite well," Amaris responded. "So, last time I was in, you were telling me a little about some of the more ancient and hard-to-find books that you've come across."

"Yes, did any of those texts interest you?" Ahsan asked.

"A couple of them, definitely," Amaris said. "Do you have anything else? Any one-of-a-kind volumes? I would be willing to pay dearly for anything like that."

"I'm afraid that anything we have like that is not for sale," Ahsan relented.

"But you do have stuff like that?" Amaris inquired. "Surely, there must be a price."

"Family heirlooms," Ahsan said. "Quite priceless. They aren't here in the store anyway, my brother Armond has them."

"I've never met your brother," Amaris replied.

"No, he is usually here with me, but has been out in California for quite some time on business."

"Well, even if they aren't for sale, I would very much like to see anything that you have," Amaris said. "I'm a sucker for unique things."

"Perhaps when he comes back I can arrange that. For now, these three volumes that you requested came in. You're already paid up, so they're all yours."

"Excellent," Amaris replied as he took the books under his arm. "I will see you soon, Ahsan. Stay well, my friend."

"You too," Ahsan said while waving as Amaris exited through the front door of the shop.

Amaris headed west from the shop and took a quick right down the nearest alleyway. After walking fifty feet, he was sure he was out of view from the roadway. He raised his left hand out in front of him and a purple-tinged portal opened in front of him. Amaris stepped inside and the portal snapped shut behind him.

"I'm getting closer," Amaris said as he stepped out into a dimly lit room. The walls were lined with desks, piled with equipment. Several computers whirred in the background. "Soon I will have the book in my hands and I can make things right. Soon this room won't be empty when I get here."

ೞ ೞ ೞ ೞ ೞ ೞ

Hayden sat in a booth across from Elle and sipped from his glass of soda. They had decided to stop in Fullerton to eat at Eduardo Quesada's. He watched as Elle took the last few bites of her burrito. The restaurant was mostly quiet, a few other patrons scattered around at other tables. Hayden glanced out the window and watched as the city's inhabitants proceeded with their daily lives. In the back of his mind, Hayden noticed the familiar creaking sound of the restaurant's front door opening and closing. He drew his attention back to the table as the new footsteps seemed to draw closer to him and Elle.

"Father?" an unfamiliar voice said.

Hayden looked up at the person, a young man, in his teens. For a moment, he considered the possibility that Dan was standing just around the corner and would pop out any second laughing. A joke perhaps.

"Sorry, you must have me mistaken for someone else," Hayden told the young man.

"Hayden," he replied. "Hayden de Vere?"

"Yeah, that's me," Hayden said. "But you're just a tad bit old to be my kid. Did Dan put you up to this?"

"My mother is Kali Henderson," the young man replied.

Elle momentarily choked on the bite of food in her mouth before recovering and washing it down with a large gulp of her soda. Her gaze then focused in on Hayden.

"Okay, I'm sorry, but Kali and I never had a child together," Hayden replied. "Besides, you're more than half my age."

____

"My name is Amaris," the young man continued. "My mother was pregnant when the Alva'ci kidnapped her."

Hayden felt his chest tighten, as if a stack of bricks had just been placed on it. He looked over at Elle to see her staring at him, eyes wide open and unblinking.

"Okay, if this is true, then how are you a teenager?" Hayden asked.

"The Alva'ci removed me from my mother's body and put me in some kind of advanced pod that sped up my development," Amaris replied. "When I woke up, I was fifteen years old already. The ship that I was on was half destroyed, but the room that my pod was in was still intact."

"Wait, you were in that back room?" Hayden said surprised. "I had no idea. I had wondered what was back there, but never got a chance to check after I confronted the Alva'ci. We should go somewhere else and continue this conversation. Our apartment isn't far from here."

The group arrived at the apartment and filtered inside. Elle joined Hayden in the kitchen while Amaris seated himself in the living room.

"This is crazy," she whispered to Hayden. "I'm not mad at you... you didn't know. But is this for real?"

"We'll see," Hayden replied. "It seems like it might be. Even so, I would take everything he says with grain of salt."

"I got you a glass of water," Elle told Amaris as she and Hayden entered the living room and sat down.

"Thank you," Amaris replied. "Just so you know, I'm not here to ruin anything. I don't want to intrude on your lives. I'm able to take care of myself. I simply wanted you guys to know that I existed. If you want to have a relationship with me beyond that, then great. If not, I understand."

"To be perfectly honest," Hayden replied. "Your story... or account of what happened, would seem unlikely if I was just some normal person. Given the circumstances, it's actually pretty reasonable. My question is, why would the Alva'ci keep a baby?"

"I don't know the answer to that," Amaris said. "Research or experimentation... that would be my guess. I'm assuming that the creature never got the chance because you showed up to fight it."

"What all do you know about the Alva'ci and what happened out there?" Hayden asked. "Or about your mother?"

"Not much," Amaris said. "The pod that I was in filled my head with basic knowledge about the world and who I was. I know what my mother looked like, I know her name, and who you are. When I woke up, I accessed the ships logs and found out what happened to the Alva'ci."

"How did you survive?" Hayden continued his questioning. "How did you get back to Earth? That ship was way out in the middle of space."

"I spent a long time in that ship alone," Amaris replied. "I searched and I read everything that I could find. It was lonely and excruciating at times. I finally accepted that I would be alone in there forever. I hate to admit it, but there were several moments that I considered just standing in the airlock and pressing that button to eject myself into space."

"That's horrible," Elle said softly.

"I couldn't bring myself to do it," Amaris said. "I didn't even have the strength and fortitude to end my own misery. Then one day I was reading through files on the ship's computer system. There were millions of files. Lots of journal-like entries from the Alva'ci. The one that I stumbled upon that day, outlined some kind of backup… a failsafe, I guess. The creature had built a one-time use portal field into my pod. I decided that anywhere that portal sent me was better than where I was, so I figured out how to activate it and jumped into it."

"It brought you here?" Hayden asked.

"It brought me to Earth," Amaris confirmed. "To a grassy field surrounded by mountains and waterfalls. I learned that place is called Yosemite. I still didn't know what to do, but I remembered the little that I knew about my mother, and you, and decided to come here."

"So what do you know about Kali?" Hayden inquired.

"I know that she died," Amaris said. "I know that she was not too much older than I am now. Her name, what she looked like, that she had a sister. That's about it. Do you know how she died?"

"She died…" Hayden paused. "She died because she was infected by a blast of power from the Alva'ci. It was too much for her. It corrupted her until things got out of control and she passed away. Her sister, Paige, was my friend. The Alva'ci killed her also."

"But you and my mother, you were together?" Amaris asked before being interrupted.

"Knock, knock!" Abby said as she opened the front door and walked in holding Kiera in her arms.

Elle looked over at Abby, her eyes communicating the message that Abby should have called before bringing the baby back to the apartment.

"Oh, I'm sorry," Abby stuttered through her words. "You guys look like you're busy. I'll take her back to my place and come back later."

"Is that your child?" Amaris asked Hayden.

"Yes, that is mine and Elle's daughter," Hayden

answered while still glaring at Abby.

"What's her name?"

"Her name is Kiera."

"It's fascinating," Amaris said. "She probably wasn't born that much later than I was. She's still an infant and I'm grown."

"Our lives are full of fascinating and odd things," Abby said, trying to break the tension in the room.

Amaris stood and walked over to Abby. Hayden breathed in deeply and readied himself to act if necessary.

"She's beautiful," Amaris said as he looked down at Kiera and touched her cheek.

"Thank you," Elle replied.

Underneath Hayden's shirt, the amulet began to faintly glow for just a moment, though it went unnoticed by everyone in the room.

"Well, I don't want to keep you any longer," Amaris declared as he turned back to face Hayden and Elle. "It looks like you two have your hands full enough with your new baby. As I said before, I am not here to insert myself into your lives. I merely wanted to reach out and let you know that I exist. However, if you are okay with getting to know each other better, I would welcome it. No pressure."

"Thank you, Amaris," Hayden replied. "I will admit

that this all caught me off-guard. I don't mean to be succinct or seem like I'm interrogating you. Give me a day to process all of this information and we can talk again."

"Okay," Amaris said, as he pulled a card from his pocket. "I am staying at this hotel for the time being. My room number is written on the back. Goodnight everyone."

෨ ෨ ෨ ෨ ෨ ෨

The next morning, Hayden decided that he would take Amaris up on his offer and visit the hotel. He had tried to convince himself that perhaps there was some truth to the story, but nevertheless he remained suspicious. It was an unfortunate consequence ingrained in his psyche by all of the recent events and tragedies that had befallen himself and those close to him.

"Babe, I'm going to head over to that hotel for a little while," he told Elle as they showered together. "I need to either ease my mind or prove myself right. Whichever happens is better than uncertainty."

"Okay," Elle replied, while keeping one ear's attention focused on the baby monitor perched on the bathroom counter. "When you get back home, maybe we can take Kiera out for a walk in the mall and grab some sandwiches at that place in the food court."

"That sounds like a great idea," Hayden said. "I won't be too long. If I don't text you within an hour of arriving there, then contact Armond and let him know where I went."

"Be careful, please," Elle said with a sigh. "I swear if you get yourself killed and make me a single mother then I'll scatter your ashes at the local landfill."

Hayden leveled his gaze at her with a smirk on his face. "You're quite adorable when you are being threatening."

Elle playfully pushed him back into the stream of water for teasing her. "I'm serious," she scolded. "You better be around to be a father to our babies."

"Babies, plural?" Hayden joked. "You already have the next one planned out? Kiera is going to get jealous if you're already trying to replace her."

"Of course, plural," Elle replied. "At the very least, one more. We can give it a year or two though before the next one."

"I'll be here," Hayden said before placing his palm on Elle's cheek and kissing her. "I promise you that. Besides, I don't seriously think that a quick visit to this hotel is going to be what does me in."

"Well, just in case," Elle said as she ran her fingers through her hair as the shower water washed the suds down her body to the drain. "If anyone ever has a gun to your head, remember this moment, with me standing here like this. That should give you the stamina to keep fighting."

"Oh, definitely," Hayden replied as he looked up and down Elle's body. "That image might even be enough to bring me back from the dead."

Elle bit her lip flirtatiously as she turned off the water. As she passed by Hayden in the shower to grab her towel, Elle brushed her body up against his.

"You know, maybe I'll just stay home with you," Hayden said, picking up on Elle's not-so-subtle cues.

"No. You're going to go," Elle replied. "I'm just teasing you. After we get home from the mall, though…"

"I better make this a quick trip then," Hayden joked. "If someone ever writes a book about all this, then you're going to be listed as my only weakness."

"As it should be," Elle said as she pulled on her underwear.

"Okay, I'll be back," Hayden told her, having already gotten completely dressed. "I love you."

Fifteen minutes later, Hayden arrived in the parking lot of the hotel Amaris said he was staying at. He looked around the exterior for signs of trouble as he headed for the front doors. Hayden bypassed the front desk and headed straight for the room number that Amaris had written on a card.

"Well, let's see if I'm right or just paranoid," Hayden said to himself as he lingered a few moments in the hallway to listen for any sounds coming from the room.

Hayden knocked on the door and waited. There was a rustle inside and then sixty seconds later Amaris opened the door.

"Hayden, I wasn't sure if you would actually come," he said.

"Neither was I," Hayden admitted. "But I thought about it overnight and decided to come by."

"Well, come inside," Amaris replied. "How are your wife and baby this morning?"

"They are well," Hayden said as he sat down on the plush chair in the corner of the room and looked around. The accommodations seemed normal, nothing nefarious stood out.

"That's good to hear," Amaris said. "Do you mind if I ask you some questions?"

"Go ahead," Hayden said. "What do you want to know?"

"I know a fair amount about my mother," Amaris stated as he sat on the edge of the bed. "The pod that I was in fed information into my mind. Mostly standard knowledge… math, language, science, and so on. It also showed me memories from my mother that the Alva'ci had somehow extracted from her consciousness. Not her entire life, but bits and pieces. Her sister, can you tell me more about her?"

"Yes. Her sister's name was Paige," Hayden replied. "She was actually my best friend for years before she died."

"I'm sorry," Amaris said. "You said her death was a result of the Alva'ci?"

"Yeah, she was killed during a vacation with her parents," Hayden said. "She wandered into a cave. The dark spirit inside the cave killed her and possessed her body.

"My mother, she was your friend also?" Amaris asked.

"I knew Kali and Paige since we were kids," Hayden answered. "Yeah, we were all friends. Your mother and I became more than friends. We dated for a short time and then she moved to another state. She came back for Paige's funeral and we met again there. We started dating again. Things were good until the Alva'ci emerged and attacked. I thought we had won, but the creature disappeared and kidnapped Kali. It took me some time to figure out how to get her back."

"You loved her though?" Amaris asked.

______

"Yeah, of course I did," Hayden said. "Very much so."

"So then, Elle?" Amaris led into a new question. "Forgive me for being blunt, but it seems like you got married to her really quickly after my mother died."

"Quite blunt," Hayden scoffed. "Elle and I have also known each other since we were younger. It's far too long a story to delve into right now and quite personal. It wasn't really as quick as it seems. There were a lot of circumstances that led to it and honestly some of them sound like they're out of a sci-fi movie. But I've known her for a long time and through a series of tragedies we grew stronger together. In the end, Elle is who I was meant to be with. But that doesn't discount the fact that your mother and I were once in love. Kali and I were just a different chapter in each other's lives."

"That makes sense," Amaris replied. "I don't want to keep you too long. Is there anything you wanted to ask me?"

"I suppose so," Hayden said. "How did you get from Yosemite to Fullerton? I assume that you knew where to look for me from your mother's memories."

"I just started walking," Amaris answered. "I think I walked for about five miles before someone offered me a ride. They dropped me off in a city called Bakersfield and gave me some money. He was very kind. I hung around there to eat and rest for several hours. Another person gave me a ride down to Brea. I got this hotel room, slept the night, and then walked the remainder of the way to meet you. I did see that restaurant in my mother's memories, so that was the first place I tried to find you."

"Now that you've met me, what are you going to do next?" Hayden asked.

"Well, I don't mean to intrude on your life," Amaris said. "I wanted to meet you. I wanted you to know that I was here. After this, I plan on exploring a little. I want to visit Washington and see where my mother went to college. I'd like to travel around a bit."

"Sounds like a fair plan," Hayden said.

"I bet you have a lot going on," Amaris said as he rose to his feet. "I'll let you get back to things. Thank you for coming by. If I make it back to Fullerton in the future, perhaps I will stop by."

"That works for me," Hayden said. "Take care of yourself. Thank you for having me over."

രു രു രു രു രു രു

Hayden held Kiera in his arm, while Elle pushed the stroller that she now regretted bringing into the mall. As the family walked past each store, Hayden pointed out pieces of bright clothing and other objects on display in the windows to their baby girl.

"If I knew you were going to carry her the entire time," Elle said to Hayden. "I would have left this thing in the car."

"Jealousy is a stinky cologne," Hayden joked back at her.

"Funny," Elle said with a mock look of disdain. "Though I actually wouldn't mind getting off my feet and having you carry me around the mall."

"Better?" Hayden asked as he placed Kiera back in the stroller and buckled her in. "I'll even push it for you."

"What a gentleman," Elle said and laughed at her own jest.

"Always, my darling," Hayden replied playfully, invoking a rough British accent.

"So how did the visit with Amaris go?" Elle asked.

"It was surprisingly uneventful," Hayden said. "He asked some questions about his mother and Paige. Pretty much just background info. I asked him about how he got down here to Orange County and what his future plans were."

"What are his plans?"

"He's apparently going to travel," Hayden replied. "Everything seemed normal to me. No signs of evil plotting. While he was talking, I used Ane'illuminus to see if he was thinking anything else or being deceitful. Everything checked out."

"Well, that's good," Elle said, relieved. "I guess we're just used to calamity, so we always expect more of it."

"Exactly," Hayden agreed. "You hungry, or did you actually want to shop for anything?"

"Oh, no, I just wanted to get Kiera out of the house and go walking around for a bit," Elle said. "We can head to the food court."

"Excellent, cause I'm crazy hungry," Hayden joked.

ᔕ ᔕ ᔕ ᔕ ᔕ ᔕ

"Okay, Kiera is down for a nap," Hayden said as he walked back into the living room. "Guess the mall really wore her out."

There was no response from Elle. Hayden scanned the room and found no sign of her. Assuming that she must have snuck past while he was laying the baby down, Hayden turned around and walked to their bedroom.

"Elle, are you in..." Hayden began but stopped mid-question.

As he entered the room, he saw a trail of Elle's clothing leading from the doorway to the bed, where she was waiting. Elle had nothing on except for a mischievous smile.

"You didn't think that I forgot about our post-mall plans, did you?" Elle asked.

"Evidently not," Hayden replied as he walked toward her.

هنا،

Chapter Five

The Book of Damnation

The familiar jingle of the bells attached to the front door of Breaker Books broke Ahsan's concentration from the stack of invoices he had been processing. He looked up to see Amaris walking into the shop with a determined stride. Amaris clenched his fists in concentration as he approached the counter.

"You will take me to your brother," Amaris stated, while focusing his mind on using the power of Ane'illuminus. "You will help me obtain the book that I have been after."

"We will go at once," Ahsan replied as he placed the stack of invoices under the counter and grabbed his coat from a nearby chair.

After a five hour flight, the duo arrived in Orange County and made their way to Fullerton. Ahsan knocked on the door of Armond's home and waited, while Amaris stood around the corner.

"Ahsan?" Armond asked startled as he opened the front door and saw his brother. "What are you doing here? Why didn't you call?"

"I need to see you," Ahsan replied. "Are the books safe?"

"Yes, they are," Armond replied, his voice now tinged with a cautious curiosity.

"Can I see them?" Ahsan asked.

"Sure," Armond said as he walked over to the bookshelf in his front room. "Here they are. Now what is this about?"

"Not those books," Ahsan said. "Powers and Practices. Is that book safe?"

Armond's brow furrowed and his demeanor changed. He spoke to Ahsan in a serious tone. "It is locked up. Why would you think it wasn't safe? What made you come all this way to check on one single book?"

"I had a vision, brother," Ahsan said. "It told me that I had to read a passage from that book. That my life was in danger."

Armond punched in the code to his safe and then pulled the book out. As he placed it on the coffee table, Ahsan walked over and sat down.

"You've never had any visions before," Armond said as he studied his brother's mannerisms.

Ahsan reached down and attempted to open the matte black cover of the ancient book. He looked over at Armond when the cover didn't budge.

"You know that there is a spell on this book preventing it from being opened unless I remove it," Armond said. "Are you in some kind of trouble, Ahsan?"

Ahsan grasped at his head as if a sharp pain had suddenly come on. "Open the book, brother," Ahsan requested in a somewhat stern tone.

"I can't do that," Armond replied flatly.

The front door of the residence flung open. The sudden crack of the splintering wood alarmed the two brothers, as they looked up to see a figure walking inside. Amaris walked over to Ahsan and forcefully pulled him up from the couch.

"We couldn't just do this the easy way, Armond?" Amaris snarled.

"Who are you?" Armond demanded. "Let go of my brother and leave us be. You have no idea what you are getting yourself into. This book is not some antique that you can hawk on the street for a quick payday."

Amaris drew a dagger from underneath his coat and

placed it against Ahsan's throat. "Remove the spell on the book," he insisted.

"I cannot," Armond replied.

Amaris pushed the blade harder. Blood began to trickle down Ahsan's neck.

"Your brother or the book?" Amaris leveled his ultimatum while pressing the blade of the dagger even harder.

"Fine," Armond relented and picked up the book from the table. "Maashus Delicus Evelium."

An aura of light rose from the book and then dissipated into the air. As Amaris watched the spectacle, Armond took the moment to telepathically reach out to Hayden for assistance. On the book's cover an inscription began to glow with fiery intensity. It read: القدرات والمهارات

"Do you even know what this book is?" Armond asked indignantly, still thinking Amaris was just a simple thief.

"Powers and Practices," Amaris replied confidently.

"Some call it Powers and Practices. We call it The Book of Damnation," Armond said, almost as if he were warning Amaris.

"Fortunately, not my damnation," Amaris snickered while releasing Ahsan from his grasp and pushing him toward his brother. "Well, it was pleasant dealing with you both, but I'm afraid that I must depart."

___

A flash of light flooded the room as Hayden stepped out of a portal, answering Armond's call for help. He looked over at Amaris with a confused expression and then over to Armond and his bleeding brother.

"Amaris, what are you doing here?" Hayden asked.

"You know this person?" Armond asked. "He is stealing one of the books of lore."

"Sorry Father, but I have to go," Amaris insisted. "I'll see you all soon."

Hayden started walking toward Amaris to stop him. Amaris drew his sword from a baldric hidden underneath his coat to keep Hayden at a distance.

"You think that will stop me?" Hayden asked sarcastically.

"It will distract you long enough for me to do this," Amaris replied as he opened a portal directly behind himself and stepped back into it.

Hayden lunged forward, but the portal snapped shut. He turned and focused his attention on Armond and Ahsan.

"Who was that and how do you know him?" Armond asked.

"That was Amaris," Hayden replied. "He is apparently my son. Kali was evidently pregnant when the Alva'ci took her. Amaris came to me a few days ago while Elle and I were eating lunch. According to his story, the Alva'ci took the baby from her body and placed it in some alien tech pod that increased his physical development. I was definitely surprised, but I didn't sense anything sinister from him when he came to me."

"Perhaps he has other powers and was shielding his true intent?" Armond mused. "We know he can open portals, so he has some abilities."

"How did I not pick up on the fact that he had powers?" Hayden asked, confused.

"Good question," Armond replied. "We don't know exactly who we're dealing with here. We also don't know why he wants that book."

"You don't have any insight into why he chose that one in particular?" Hayden asked skeptically. "Isn't that the one that you keep locked up and never open?"

"Fine, I'll explain," Armond said begrudgingly. "That book is called Powers and Practices. Abbas compiled it shortly before his death. It tells the tale of how humans first acquired the various powers. It goes into detail about the uses of each power from the simple to the advanced. The book has an entire chapter dedicated to the practice of Ane'illuminus. Another chapter details the Forbidden Spell and tells the story of all the people who attempted to use it, all unsuccessfully."

"Is that all?" Hayden replied. "That doesn't seem insanely dangerous."

"No, that's not all," Armond relented. "There is a large portion of the book that talks about Bilv'at and her powers. It is from her that the ancestors of Abbas and the other villagers learned spells related to time. With her knowledge, they were able to extend their lifetimes far beyond a normal human lifespan. There are several more of Bilv'at's spells included in the text as well. That is probably the most dangerous material in the book."

"So who exactly is Bilv'at?" Hayden asked. "Those villagers learned all that from one woman?"

"Bilv'at is not a simple human woman," Armond replied. "It is rumored that she is what is known as a Principality. A malevolent spirit that wields considerable power. I don't know, for certain, exactly what she is though. I do know that she assumed the form of a human woman while on Earth. She is extremely powerful. Bilv'at was the original Amira al-Dahr. Some ancients worshiped her as a deity."

"What happened to her?"

"According to what she told the ancestors of Abbas, her power was bound to this universe as a form of punishment," Armond explained. "As you know, when Abbas came up with and cast the rending spell to render the Alva'ci comatose in 54,000 BC, it eliminated the use of the powers amongst humans. An unforeseen consequence was that the spell also rendered Bilv'at's powers useless. The spells that Abbas and the others had used to extend their lifespans were canceled. Bilv'at also became subject to death."

"So if Bilv'at's powers are gone, then what is there to worry about?" Hayden asked.

"Well, all of the powers were gone," Armond answered. "...until you came along. The appearance of the cognizant one meant the return of the powers. Bilv'at's powers manifested in Kali until you gained possession of them. You have no idea what those powers can do and I am not inclined to teach you. They are too powerful, too dangerous. If Amaris possesses any of Kali's latent powers, then he may be able to use that book to do great harm."

"So how do we stop him?" Hayden asked.

"We need to get that book back," Armond said. "Before he has a chance to learn things. We don't know the full extent of his current powers. Obviously, he can create portals. Based on his manipulation of Ahsan, I would venture to say that he can use Ane'illuminus, at least at the rudimentary level. There's no modern precedent, but in the days of Abbas, the powers could pass down from parent to child."

"Oh great," Hayden said. "So my little baby girl Kiera

is going to start randomly lighting things on fire or using mind control to get out of cleaning her bedroom?"

"Back in the ancient times, the powers never manifested in a child until they hit puberty," Armond answered. "So you have some time to teach her responsibility, morals, and control."

"Okay," Hayden sighed in relief. "Anyway, I cannot sense Amaris anywhere. So do we just wait to see if he reappears?"

"Keep trying to find him," Armond instructed. "In the meantime, we prepare. It will take him a while to get through that entire book. I am going to get my brother bandaged up and help him get on a flight to New York."

ↄↄ ↄↄ ↄↄ ↄↄ ↄↄ ↄↄ

Hayden arrived back at home and informed Elle of what had happened with Amaris and Armond.

"I get the Ane'illuminus powers being passed down," Hayden said to Elle. "But the ability to create portals was not a power of the agents of fate. I learned how to do that after creating the amulet. It was a power of the Alva'ci."

"So, logically, Amaris shouldn't be able to create portals," Elle replied, half as a statement and half as a question.

"Not unless there's more to it," Hayden replied. "I need to go into the dreamscape and talk to the Alva'ci. It made absolutely no mention of Amaris before."

"Do you think that Amaris was some sort of revenge plan by the Alva'ci?" Elle asked.

"Perhaps," Hayden agreed. "There's definitely something that the creature is hiding from me."

"Okay, I'm going to feed Kiera," Elle replied. "Don't be gone too long."

Hayden nodded in agreement and sat down on the couch. He closed his eyes and fell back into the cushions, waking in the dreamscape. He hadn't bothered to create an elaborate scene. The ground was basic concrete pavement with no visible landscape. The sky just a blanket of darkness. Hayden called out across the expanse to the orb. As he waited for the entity to appear, Hayden noticed that small cracks of light were forming in the darkness far off in the distance. "That's not normal," he said to himself.

"You beckoned?" the orb said as it appeared and drew Hayden's attention back to what he had come for.

"I did," Hayden confirmed. "The child in the other room on your ship. You conveniently forgot to mention the fact that you snatched a baby from Kali's body."

"That's not entirely true," the orb replied. "Yes, I

never told you about that. I never promised complete transparency, though I have assisted you with knowledge when you needed it. Before my death, I figured that the rest of my ship would soon disintegrate, destroying the child. It wasn't worth mentioning. However, snatching a baby from Kali's body is not what happened."

"Then what did happen?" Hayden asked impatiently.

"Kali was not pregnant when I took her," the orb said. "When we arrived at my ship and I rendered her unconscious, I began my examination and experimentation. One of the things that I discovered was that she'd recently had intercourse. There was still genetic material from a male inside her body. Your genetic material. I extracted some of that, along with an egg from one of her ovaries. I was the last known member of my species. In an effort to end our extinction, I experimented with the idea of a hybrid lifeform. I fertilized the egg with your genetic material and then injected Alva'ci DNA into the embryo also."

"So Amaris is part Alva'ci also?" Hayden asked, the astonishment and disbelief evident in his voice.

"Yes, the DNA of my species successfully bound to the developing genetic structures," the orb confirmed.

"That explains his ability to open portals," Hayden mused.

"So the child lived and has abilities?" the orb asked.

"Yeah, the child, Amaris, is a teenager now," Hayden said. "He stole a book from Armond."

"The pod that the child was in fed him vast amounts of knowledge during his development," the orb said. "Including memories and stories that I extracted from his mother's mind. I wouldn't be surprised if he was using that book to either extract revenge or to try and save her."

"Save her? Kali is dead," Hayden said.

"That is what you told everyone else," the orb replied. "But she's not dead, not quite."

"If anyone was able to wake her, she would bleed out in an instant," Hayden said. "Saving her is something that I doubt even I could do."

"There are powers in this universe greater than you," the orb warned.

"So I've heard," Hayden said. "How do I find and stop Amaris?"

"Stop searching for just a human," the orb advised. "He is part Alva'ci. Use the amulet to search for remnants of me."

Hayden grasped the amulet and focused his thoughts. "He isn't in the present," Hayden declared. "He's in the future."

"He must have some remnants of Kali's powers if he's

traveling between then and now," the orb said. "Either you go after him or you wait for him to come back."

"If I go to him, it will take me years to get back here to the present," Hayden said, his tone defeated. "I cannot be away from Elle and the baby that long."

"Evidently, Amaris isn't spending years coming back to the present every time," the orb concluded. "I'm assuming that this visit was not his first one. You should start your preparations by trying to figure out how he is accomplishing that because it is likely that you will have to chase after him."

"Okay," Hayden sighed. "Things can never just be peaceful and quiet, can they?"

"I'll assume that was rhetorical," the orb replied. "Be forewarned, if you go dabbling in time, you may run into some of these entities that possess power you've never seen. Not all of them are evil, but those that are…"

"I understand," Hayden said. "I'll try to avoid getting killed and ending the world. I should be getting back to reality now. Goodbye."

Hayden awoke on the couch in his living room. Elle was sitting in the chair across from him, breastfeeding Kiera.

"That was quick," Elle remarked. "You were only gone about ten minutes."

"How are you two doing?" Hayden asked.

"Good," Elle replied. "She's hungry. Did you find out what you were looking for?"

"Somewhat," Hayden answered. "The orb pretty much confirmed Amaris' story, with a few corrections. Kali wasn't pregnant, the Alva'ci created an embryo and infused its own DNA into it. Amaris is also part Alva'ci. That explains the portals. It turns out that Amaris is in the future right now, so there's a new obstacle to overcome."

"I know this sounds selfish, but don't go," Elle said. "I can't bear to have you gone, wondering the entire time if I'll ever see you again… if Kiera will ever see her father."

"I'm not going," Hayden assured her. "He's a lot further in the future than we were. It would take me at least twelve years to get back here to the present. I don't think my mind could handle twelve years alone in the dreamscape on the journey back. There must be answers somewhere else. The orb alluded that Amaris must have found a way to shorten how long it takes to travel backward in time. I have to figure something out because I don't think he's just going to let us all live in peace."

"She's asleep," Elle whispered while nodding down toward Kiera. "Do you want to lay her down in the crib for a nap?"

Hayden took the baby and gently rocked her as he walked down the hall to the bedroom. Elle walked in a few seconds behind him.

"I just want to be done with powers and wars and strife," Hayden said to Elle as he placed Kiera in the crib. "I just want to stop and raise this amazing little baby with you."

"Me too," Elle agreed. "Soon, babe. Soon."

❧ ❧ ❧ ❧ ❧ ❧

The morning lingered on as the group sat around in Armond's living room. Hayden repeatedly went into the dreamscape to try and figure out how Amaris had managed to speed up the time travel process. Each time that Hayden came out of the construct he was more frustrated by his inability to come up with an adequate solution. The rest of the group spent the morning in conversation, pausing only to offer Hayden words of support and to pitch an occasional idea.

"I don't know what I'm missing," he told the group after his final attempt. "I need more knowledge. Perhaps tomorrow I can try again."

Hayden stood in front of the fridge in Armond's kitchen. He grabbed a couple of sodas for Elle and himself. The rest of the group was still engaged in conversation in the living room. Abby sat on the couch, holding Kiera in her arms, gently swaying back and forth to keep her asleep as everyone talked around her. Hayden rounded the corner, cans of soda in hand.

With a blinding flash of light, Amaris stepped forth from a portal near where Elle and Dan were seated. His sword was already drawn and at the ready. The cans of soda fell from Hayden's hands and hit the carpet as he immediately began hurtling streams of concentrated electric current at Amaris. His son appeared to be absorbing the energy from Hayden's attacks.

"Up!" Amaris shouted at Elle. "Get up now or this sword goes through that baby and the girl holding it."

Hayden began walking toward the group. Elle hesitated for a brief moment, but then quickly rose to her feet.

"Elle, don't!" Hayden shouted as he closed the distance between them.

Amaris grabbed Elle by the arm and jerked her body backward through the portal with him. Hayden fell to his knees on the carpet as the portal snapped shut where Elle had just stood, moments ago.

"Fuck! Not again," Hayden yelled. He clenched his fists and the ground began to shake beneath the house as a symbol of power glowed on the back of his right hand.

"Hey bro, you'll get her back," Dan said, as he placed his hand on Hayden's shoulder in an attempt to calm him down. "You always prevail. You always end up winning."

"Ask Kali if she thinks I won last time this happened," Hayden countered. "Ask Tiffany, Mackenzie, or Lora. Oh wait, we can't ask any of them. I ended up winning, but they're all dead."

"Okay, that's fair," Dan replied. "But we know a lot more now than we did back then. We are prepared. You can do this."

"If Elle dies," Hayden began as he rose to his feet and looked Dan in the eyes. "If she dies, I'll let the world burn."

"Well, then for all our sakes, let's make sure that doesn't happen," Dan said grimly.

Abby stood and rocked the baby, who had woken and started crying from all the commotion. Hayden looked over at Kiera and took a deep breath to calm himself.

"I'm going after him," Hayden declared. "I don't have time to wait for us to figure out how to shorten backward time travel. I'll just have to hope that I discover that secret while I'm in the future."

"You don't think you need to prepare?" Abby asked in a hushed voice as she continued rocking Kiera. "We don't even know the extent of Amaris' powers. He was able to withstand your attack. Are you sure that an all out one-on-one battle is a good idea when he has Elle at his mercy?"

Hayden paused for a moment to contemplate the truth of what Abby had said. Amaris would definitely use Elle as a way to put Hayden at a disadvantage.

"I need an advantage," Hayden admitted. "I won't be going alone."

الآن

Chapter Six

The Daughter of Elle

Abby looked at Hayden, the confusion on her face was shared by everyone else in the group. She looked down to see that Kiera had finally fallen back asleep.

"Who would you take with you that would be of any use?" Abby asked.

"No," Armond interjected. "I know what you're thinking, Hayden."

"You also know that I never end up listening to your objections when times are desperate," Hayden told Armond. "Yet things always seem to work out."

"Okay, true, but this is unprecedented," Armond countered. "She's a baby. You don't know what effects this will have on her in the long term."

Abby's eyes widened as her glance alternated between

Hayden and Kiera. "What are you talking about?"

"Give me my daughter, Abby," Hayden instructed as he walked toward her.

"No…" Abby stuttered as she took a step back and held Kiera tighter. Jared stood up from his place on the couch as if to confront Hayden. He immediately returned to his seat when Hayden glared at him.

"Give me my daughter," Hayden's voice commanded again, this time seeming to echo with several different octaves at once. Abby held Kiera out for Hayden to take her.

"You're crossing lines, Hayden," Armond warned, knowing that the distinct change in Hayden's voice meant that he had just pushed that command into Abby's mind using the power of Ane'illuminus.

"Maybe if I crossed more lines then dozens of people we knew wouldn't be dead," Hayden replied.

Armond shook his head and watched as Hayden placed Kiera on the living room carpet and draped a blanket over her body.

"I still don't understand what's happening," Dan said. "How is a baby going to help you fight?"

"You'll see in a minute," Hayden replied.

"You're still going to be delayed going after Amaris," Armond said, attempting one last round of reasoning to dissuade Hayden from his course of action. "You'll have to prepare her and train her."

"I've already made my decision, Armond," Hayden replied as he knelt down on the carpet next to Kiera and held his hands over her body. As he closed his eyes the amulet sprang to life, emitting a bright purple hue. "Aspiris Dasfiya Sitta 'Ashar."

The entire group watched in anticipation as scattered bursts of light appeared throughout the living room and then appeared to weave themselves into a strand of particles above Kiera's body. After a blinding flash of purple light, everyone looked down at Kiera.

"Holy shit," Dan mumbled in disbelief.

Hayden watched as Kiera opened her eyes. He adjusted the blanket around her as she sat up. The infant that had been lying on the carpet was now a sixteen-year-old girl. Armond shook his head again, half in disapproval and half in astonishment that Hayden had actually pulled off the feat. Kiera attempted to speak, but no words came to her. She clutched Hayden, pulling his arms around her body, as if seeking a familiar safe space.

"It's okay, baby girl, I've got you," Hayden told her. Hayden pressed the tips of his fingers against Kiera's temple and closed his eyes. Their bodies fell limp onto the carpet.

"...and he's gone off to the dreamscape," Dan said.

ↂ ↂ ↂ ↂ ↂ ↂ

Kiera and Hayden woke in a serene landscape within the dreamscape. As Hayden placed his palm on Kiera's forehead, he looked up and noticed the same cracks of light permeating the sky as he had seen before. This time they had appeared on the horizon above a picturesque waterfall far in the distance. Once again, he didn't have time to worry about the strange occurrence.

"Let's teach you some things, baby girl," Hayden said as he closed his eyes and concentrated.

Kiera's eyelids fluttered intensely as if she were locked in the throes of a vivid dream. Hayden poured knowledge into her mind. Everything that he could think of that was relevant to her ability to live and function.

"Dad," Kiera said as she finally opened her eyes. "I can talk. I know things. I'm…"

"You're ready to continue," Hayden said. "I'm sorry that I had to age you up, but I don't think that I can fight this battle alone. I will need your help to rescue your mother."

"You created all this?" Kiera said. "The whole scene around us."

"Yes," Hayden confirmed. "You should be able to do this also. I want you to try."

Hayden waved his hand in front of himself and the endless fields of lush greenery disappeared. The dreamscape became nothing more than a blank canvas of darkness. The only thing that persisted were the cracks of light in the distant sky.

"Go ahead," Hayden urged. "Create something. It doesn't have to be the same as what I had. Use your imagination."

Kiera focused her thoughts. Hayden marveled as things began to take shape around them. Flat grey concrete appeared under their feet, followed by elaborate brickwork walls around them. As the scene continued to come into being, Hayden noticed that they were standing in a train station. He could smell a mixture of oil, floor cleaners, and yeast hanging in the still air.

"Amazing," Hayden said as a train pulled into the station. "Okay, I would say that you have this power down pretty good. Let's try something else."

Kiera smiled as she observed the world that she had called into existence around them. "Okay, I'm ready."

As they went through each of Hayden's powers, they found that Kiera had access to each of the Elemental powers, including Fire, Earth, Air, and Water. Among the sub-elemental powers, she was only able to conjure the power of Electricity. Her use of Ane'illuminus was evident by her ability to control the dreamscape, but she was unable to cast any of the Seven Spells. After Kiera practiced her execution and control, the duo concluded her training.

"Very good," Hayden admonished. "You're a quick learner."

"I'm sure most of it is inherited talent," Kiera joked.

"Well, you learned to use and control the Powers at least as quickly as I did, if not more so," Hayden said. "So don't be modest about your abilities and potential. You have every right to be confident. I'm proud of you. Just remember, you are responsible for what you do when you use these powers."

"Thank you, Dad," Kiera said, her joking grin now turning to a soft smile.

Hayden knelt down as he saw a small black cat saunter out of the traincar and walk toward him. The cat rubbed against Hayden's outstretched hand as it neared.

"Cute cat," Hayden said as he looked up at Kiera.

"I actually didn't make any cats," Kiera admitted, confused by the feline's random appearance.

"You didn't?" Hayden asked, the concern in his voice

evident. "Things don't just appear in the dreamscape. Something isn't quite right. It's like someone else is breaking through, but that would almost be like breaking into my mind. It shouldn't be possible. Once we get your mother back, I need to figure out what is going on."

"Do you think that it's Amaris doing it?" Kiera asked.

"I don't think so," Hayden replied. "If it were him, I would assume things would be much less subtle. This almost seems like an attempt at communication."

ო ო ო ო ო ო

A few minutes later, Kiera and Hayden woke. He helped her to her feet and opened a portal, which the duo stepped through. They reappeared after another five minutes, with Kiera now dressed in some of Elle's clothes.

"Hi everyone," Kiera said as the portal closed behind her and Hayden.

"Umm, hi Kiera," Abby said. "I was just rocking you to sleep a few minutes ago."

"I know this must be really weird for all of you," Kiera said. "My dad and I spent some time in the dreamscape and he taught me everything that I need to know. He told me all about every one of you."

"You guys were only out for a few minutes," Dan said.

"It was several days on the inside," Hayden replied. "We had to spend some time on developing her powers to an acceptable level."

"So, she can do the things that you can do?" Jared asked.

"Not everything, but Kiera has several of the powers," Hayden said.

"Keep her safe, Hayden," Abby interjected.

"Of course, I will," Hayden replied. "We can stay for a meal, but then we should be off."

"I will prepare something for everyone," Armond said. "Not to be a constant voice of dissent, but you still haven't figured out how Amaris decreased the time it takes to travel backwards in time. If you go and cannot solve that problem…"

"Then it will take us twelve and a half years to get back here to the present," Hayden finished Armond's sentence. "Let's hope I can figure out that solution while Kiera and I are in 2049."

"Yes, twelve and a half years, assuming that you all survive that long of a trip in the dreamscape," Armond added. "That is a very long time to be under."

"Wait, I'll be twenty-eight when we get back here?"

Kiera asked, shocked at the news.

"Not if I can find out how Amaris is coming back in time," Hayden replied. "From what I can tell, he is traveling twenty-five years in only about one week's time. If it's any consolation, even if it took us twelve and a half years, you would still physically look sixteen."

"That's not super consoling," Kiera said.

"I know. I'll figure it out," Hayden told her. "Everything will work out. Your mother and I were stuck in the future with no clue how to get back. It took us a few months of research, but we figured it out. We can do it again."

"Physical appearance and age isn't what I'm worried about," Armond said. "It's the effects on everyone's mental state that I'm worried about. As you recall Hayden, Elle felt mildly out of place after only two years of time travel back to the present."

"Yeah, I know. That's why I'll figure out a way," Hayden replied. "If I keep doing this then soon I'm going to be ninety years old in a twenty-something body."

"And locked up in an asylum," Dan joked. "You better make it all work out, buddy."

න න න න න න

In the dark depths of outer space, a bright flash of orange ripped through the silence as Hayden and Kiera's portal appeared near the planet Moira. As they exited the portal, Kiera looked around in wonder at the nearby planets and the glow of the supermassive black hole.

"It's amazing," Kiera said.

"It truly is something else to see," Hayden concurred. "Let's get comfortable down on that planet. We have to spend twelve-and-a-half hours inside this gravitational field to have the time dilation advance us to the year 2049."

Hayden opened another portal that transported them to the surface of Moira. Kiera soon found that the mention of comfort was something her father was saying in relativistic terms, as the planet's surface was mostly barren and inhospitable. They sat on the dust-covered ground and waited.

"Mother has been to this planet before, right?" Kiera asked, remembering one of the stories that her father told her in the dreamscape during her training.

"Yes, we were brought here by Kali," Hayden confirmed.

"Kali is Amaris' mother," Kiera continued. "She fought you here. She didn't like my mom, huh?"

"Correct," Hayden replied with a chuckle, noting the

simplistic explanation. "Kali was once a very close friend of mine. She was even once a girlfriend of mine. The Alva'ci kidnapped her and she became corrupted with its power. In that sense she was a victim. However, even considering the fact that her mind was corrupted, she still did some things that were unforgivable. For example, trying to kill your mother."

"That's kind of sad though," Kiera thought out loud. "If I wasn't myself and did some things that I regretted, I would hope for forgiveness."

"You're my daughter, Kiera," Hayden said. "It's different."

"So even if Kali went back to normal and asked for forgiveness, you wouldn't do it?" Kiera asked.

"Kali is dead," Hayden replied.

"No she's not," Kiera said. "Your thoughts are saying that she's not dead."

"Do not read my thoughts, child," Hayden said sternly. "As I told you in the dreamscape, you must practice responsibility and ethics when using your powers. That being said, I apologize for not being completely honest with you. It is true, Kali is barely alive. For all intents and purposes though, she is basically dead. If she woke, she would die in seconds from her wounds. I don't know if it was a moment of weakness and stupidity or a noble act, but at the time, I couldn't bring myself to just watch her die in front of me. She's hidden away and in suspended animation, so as far as anyone else is concerned, she's dead."

Kiera contemplated Hayden's response for a few seconds. "I promise not to read your thoughts if you promise to be honest with me."

"Okay, baby girl, you've got yourself a deal," Hayden replied.

"I'm not a baby anymore, Dad," Kiera said.

"Well, you were still a baby just a few hours ago," Hayden replied. "...and you're always my baby girl."

"You didn't answer my original question," Kiera said.

"About forgiving Kali?" Hayden said, recalling the query. "It's complicated. I do hold a grudge. She put you and your mother in great danger. She killed a lot of people. To be perfectly honest, I just don't know if I have it in me to forgive her."

"I understand," Kiera replied. "Do you think that's why Amaris kidnapped Mom? To get back at you?"

"Perhaps," Hayden admitted. "I wouldn't be surprised if he blames me for Kali's death, or near-death, rather. He may be using your mother to lure me into a trap to get revenge."

———

"We're going to save her though, right," Kiera asked. "You won't let anything bad happen to her? I want her to see me all grown up now."

"Oh, well she's going to be surprised to see you suddenly sixteen years old, that's for sure," Hayden said. "We will save her. I promise you that."

As the hours passed, Hayden and Kiera walked along the desolate landscape of the planet, looking in vain for variations to the dust and rock that littered the surface. Eventually, Hayden looked at his watch and drew in a deep breath.

"It's finally time to go," he declared. "Prepare yourself mentally. I have no idea what the world is going to look like when we step out the other side of the portal. It may be okay or it could be a wasteland. We may have to fight immediately, so prepare yourself."

"Okay, I'm ready," Kiera said.

"Hey, I love you," Hayden added.

The orange glow of the portal reflected against their faces as it opened. Hayden took Kiera by the hand and they walked through into the unknown.

〜 〜 〜 〜 〜 〜

Amaris paced around the dingy room, lost in thought. Elle sat quietly in the corner watching him, handcuffed to the highly uncomfortable metal chair. Her back ached and her tailbone felt like it was on fire from being confined in the same spot for several hours. Amaris stopped for a moment and then walked back over to the desk, thumbing through the pages of Powers and Practices.

"You've read those pages a million times," Elle taunted. "Do you think some new information is going to magically appear this time?"

"Shut up, Elle," Amaris snapped back. "I was trying to figure out a way to do this without killing you, but if you insist on me cutting corners then I can certainly do that."

Amaris walked up to the chair and unlocked the handcuffs from one of Elle's wrists. As he pulled her up from the chair, Elle found that her legs were not ready to be put into action so quickly. She stumbled as the numb stinging sensation radiated through her lower extremities.

"Stand up!" Amaris demanded as he pulled her along toward the wall.

He pulled Elle's arms up over her head and slipped the open cuff through a thick metal bracket protruding from the wall about six feet above the floor. Amaris secured the open cuff around Elle's free wrist and walked back over to the desk to continue reading.

"...and I thought being stuck in that chair was bad," Elle thought to herself.

"I need more power to accomplish my goals," Amaris spoke to Elle with his back still to her. "You are going to help me get that."

"How am I going to help you?" Elle replied sarcastically. "Maybe you made a mistake here, I have no powers."

"You have no powers," Amaris confirmed as he turned around and walked toward Elle. "Yes, that makes you easy to control. Yet, you have exactly what I need. You and Hayden are linked. He cast the Forbidden Spell on himself and you. Your souls are intertwined, the link between the two of you is extraordinary. So, yes, you have *everything* I need."

"What are you going to do to me?" Elle asked, her voice now slightly shaky.

Amaris ignored her question and walked back over to the desk for one last glance at the book. "You'll see soon enough."

Elle writhed in discomfort as the handcuffs dug in to her wrists and her arms began to ache. Amaris once again approached her and placed his hands on the sides of her head. The lights in the room flickered as he concentrated. Elle continued to struggle.

"E'it Talavas Hosem," he muttered as he closed his eyes and focused his powers.

Elle took the opportunity to fight back. She sunk her teeth into Amaris' forearm and bit down as hard as she could manage. He lunged back in pain, with blood running down his arm from the wound. Elle attempted to kick him, but he was quickly out of reach. The stinging sensation of the handcuffs digging deeper into her wrists sent a sharp pain throughout her body.

"Stupid," Amaris snarled, anger readily visible in his eyes, as he drew his sword from his side and pointed it at Elle.

As Amaris stepped forward, Elle instantly regretted her poorly thought out attack. He drew the tip of the sword up to Elle's neck and pressed it against her skin. She attempted to hold her breath, but the building fear resulted in short panicked breaths instead.

Amaris lightly ran the blade's tip from Elle's neck to her waist. As hard as she tried, Elle could not still her body from involuntarily trembling. Amaris tucked the sword's edge under the hem of her shirt and quickly pulled it upward, slicing the fabric with deft precision. Elle shuddered as she looked down, fully expecting to see a resulting laceration. She slowly began to calm down when she saw that there was no blood, no horrible wound, just exposure. Her shirt, cut right up the middle, hung from her shoulders, exposing her bra and bare stomach. Amaris resheathed his sword.

"Understand me," Amaris said in a low and menacing voice. "If you do anything like that again, I will not be so nice to you. The rest of those clothes will come off. I can, and I will, do unspeakable things to you. I don't want to have to waste time forcing you into submission, but I will if you force me to. Are we clear?"

"Yes," Elle replied, her voice broken through her still panicked breathing.

"Good," Amaris said, his voice now decidedly more chipper. "Let's begin again."

As he walked up to Elle, Amaris placed his palms against her chest. He looked into her eyes as he once again chanted the same phrase. "E'it Talavas Hosem."

Elle felt a dull pain building in her chest. The flicker of the room's lights made the gradually building glow of light surrounding Amaris' hands more apparent. Elle started to breath deeply as an intense heat began to accompany the rising pain. It flowed throughout her body as if it were in her bloodstream. Amaris pressed his palms harder against her chest and Elle began to convulse in pain. She screamed until her voice cracked and faltered.

"Just a little more," Amaris yelled over Elle's shrieks.

Sweat began to pour down Elle's body as she continued to violently convulse. She choked on her own desperate attempts to gasp for breath. Blood from her bound wrists streamed down her arms. Amaris' hands glowed with brilliant light. Against his palms he could feel Elle's heartbeat, now tachycardic. The crushing pain was unbearable and Elle could feel consciousness beginning to slip away from her.

As a vignette of darkness was building on the periphery of Elle's vision, Amaris finally withdrew his hands from her chest. The overwhelming pain subsided, replaced by a persistent ache that permeated every muscle in her body. Slowly, her heartrate and breathing normalized.

"See, that wasn't too bad," Amaris said with a malevolent smile on his face. "Didn't take that long and your heart didn't give out."

"Are you doing this to me as revenge for Hayden killing your mother?" Elle asked, her voice raspy from dehydration.

"Revenge?" Amaris said. "Perhaps partially. But I have larger aspirations than vengeance. Besides, my mother isn't dead."

"She died in space, Amaris," Elle said.

"Is that what Hayden told all of you?" Amaris

countered. "She is mortally wounded, but she is alive. I have seen her. Hayden used his powers to put her in a coma and hide her away on some distant planet. I suppose that she's close enough to dead though, if she were to ever wake she would likely die in seconds."

Elle was silent. Amaris studied her reaction for a few moments before walking back over to the desk. He closed the book and placed it into a safe.

"Are you mad that Hayden didn't tell you that Kali wasn't actually dead?" Amaris asked as he approached Elle. "Feeling a little animosity that you need to take care of?"

"No, it's fine," she angrily replied.

"Doesn't seem like it's fine," Amaris snickered. "Since all that unpleasant business went so much better than expected, there's plenty of time for me to make good on other threats."

"Just leave me be, please," Elle said.

"You know, Elle," Amaris replied, completely ignoring her request. "When Hayden visited me at that hotel in Orange County, he was a little distracted it seemed. We spent the time talking about the past. Just a normal conversation. However, this image kept flashing into his mind. An image of you... in the shower. I could see why he was distracted. It was quite enticing. In fact, I wouldn't mind seeing that in person."

Elle's breathing shallowed as Amaris' index finger slipped under the bridge of her bra and she realized what he meant. She started to raise her right leg up to kick Amaris back. His free hand immediately gripped the hilt of his sword. "Do you not remember what I said about attacking me?" he asked forcefully.

Amaris removed his coat and flung it over the metal chair that he previously had Elle restrained in. Hooking his finger back around the bridge of her bra, Amaris tugged down on it for a moment and then traced his finger down her stomach to the waistband of her jeans.

"Amaris, don't do this," Elle warned. "You accomplished what you wanted to, now just let me go."

"Let you go?" he replied mockingly. "Go where? It's 2049 and the planet is a wasteland. Even if you manage to find some survivors out there, they'll do far worse to you and they'll do it over and over again until you wish you were dead."

"Then just leave me alone," Elle said.

Amaris ignored her plea and hooked his finger around the button of her pants. His other hand reached around to her back and grasped the clasp of her bra.

"Stop!" Elle demanded.

The dull grey of the concrete wall behind Elle lit

up with the reflection of a bright orange light. Amaris looked over his shoulder to see Hayden step out of a portal, accompanied by a teenage girl.

المستقبل

Chapter Seven

The End of All Things

As the portal snapped shut behind Hayden and Kiera, Amaris took his hands off Elle and turned to face the duo. Kiera watched in amazement as her father immediately sprang into action. Hayden grasped the amulet and it began to brilliantly shine. Waves of energy flowed outward from his body.

Amaris fired off a quick, but powerful, blast of energy at Hayden who deflected it into a nearby wall. Hayden clenched his fist and a symbol of power lit on the back of his hand. The metal handcuffs restraining Elle to the bracket on the concrete wall disintegrated into dust. Elle fell forward onto the ground in exhaustion.

The back of Hayden's hands now cycled through several symbols of power. His expression conveyed the feeling of rage that was coursing through his mind. He swept his hand out in front of him and a massive shockwave of energy obliterated the walls of the building, sending debris hundreds of yards across the surrounding landscape. The remainder of the building crumbled and dust rose into the dreary grey sky like smoke. Amaris stepped away from Elle and Kiera took the opportunity to run over and help her mother.

"Mom, I got you," Kiera said as she helped her sit up.

"Kiera?" Elle asked, the surprise apparent in her voice and in her expression. "How are you... What happened? You're just a baby though... how old are you?"

"I'm sixteen," Kiera said as she grabbed a dingy piece of cloth from the ground and used it to wipe away the blood from Elle's arms.

"Are you okay?" Hayden yelled to Elle while keeping an eye on Amaris. "Did he hurt you?"

"I'll be okay, just a little beat up," Elle replied.

"Shall we?" Amaris asked, taunting Hayden toward the inevitable fight.

"What do you hope to accomplish?" Hayden replied. "You don't seriously think that you can win, do you?"

"Well, your wife was kind enough to let me channel some of your power through her connection with you," Amaris said. "So, I think you'll find me much more of a challenge than you anticipated."

Amaris fired off a continuous stream of energy from his palm toward Hayden, who met it with his own. The dueling streams locked in a stalemate in between the two. Hayden looked over at Kiera and met her gaze. Kiera understood and rose to her feet, hitting Amaris from behind with an infusion of fire and electricity. Elle looked up at her daughter in amazement, shocked to see that she also had powers.

Hayden's energy blast began to gain an edge over Amaris' as Kiera continued her auxiliary assault. Amaris looked over his shoulder and swept his free hand through the air in Kiera's direction, knocking her from her feet to the ground. He closed his eyes and pushed a series of thoughts into Kiera's mind.

"Kiera, get up!" Hayden yelled to her over the crackling noises of the ensuing battle. "Help me!"

"I can't do that." she replied in a docile voice as she sat down next to Elle.

The amulet pulsed with a bright flash and Hayden intensified his attack. Amaris' energy blast dissipated in the midst of Hayden's increased effort. Amaris flew back through the air as Hayden's attack finally landed and his body skidded across the ground for several feet after making impact.

As Amaris rose to his feet, Hayden prepared himself. His hands pulsed with energy. The temperature around the now-destroyed building dropped suddenly. Hayden fired off a bolt of electrical current, which Amaris deflected into a nearby automobile.

"See, I'm not some weak child," Amaris said defiantly.

"What did you do to Kiera?" Hayden demanded to know.

"I wouldn't worry about her," Amaris replied as he walked forward and used his powers to hurtle boulders at Hayden.

Hayden deflected the incoming projectiles one by one, each exploding into a cloud of dust as they hit various objects. Father and son continued to go back and forth, firing off volleys of attacks against each other. The fight was beginning to wear on both of them.

"Need a break, old man?" Amaris taunted.

"You've got to be kidding me," Hayden said, holding back laughter.

"Why don't you just grab your pretty little wife and your child and go home?" Amaris replied. "I've got what I need. I'll do my thing and you can do yours."

"I don't think so," Hayden answered. "I'm sure that would just equal me having to take care of this sometime in the future. Might as well end this now."

"Like you *took care of* my mother?" Amaris replied sarcastically. "For someone who professed to love her so much, you sure were quick to choose the option of stabbing her."

"You don't know what you're talking about," Hayden rebuked.

"I know what I saw. I know that you had a million other options," Amaris said. "You took the easy way out and eliminated my mother so that you could replace her with Elle."

"That's not what happened," Hayden said. "Everything was split-second decisions, no time to think or weigh the options. It was all reactionary. What happened was the difference between saving the planet or saving your mother. I know that sounds coldly utilitarian, but there was literally nothing I could do."

"Well Father, let me take care of Elle like you took care of Kali," Amaris snapped back as he approached Elle and Kiera.

"Do not harm her!" Hayden yelled as he sprinted toward Amaris and prepared to attack again.

Amaris grabbed Elle by the hair and pulled her to her feet. Hayden was closing in the distance between them quickly. Amaris drew his sword and began to thrust the blade toward Elle. Kiera still sat on the ground, watching the events unfold in an eerily calm manner.

Hayden's sprint came to an abrupt halt as he saw the blade cutting through the air, its collision with Elle's body imminent. He clutched the amulet and focused all his energy and rage. The stone erupted in a purple light that flowed around his body. The trajectory of the sword slowed to a near-standstill as time all but stopped.

Focusing his energy on the fight, Amaris tapped in to the remnants of Kali's powers that he had received, giving him limited range of motion free of the time freeze. It was all he needed to attack Hayden with one hand. Amaris fired off an enormous stream of energy at his father, who met it with one of his own.

The stalemate went back and forth. Hayden slowly started losing ground due to the intense focus that was required to keep time frozen in place and prevent Elle from being stabbed. Before long, Amaris' attacks started to land. Hayden concentrated and appeared to be physically unfazed.

Suddenly, Amaris halted his attack for a brief moment. He swept his hand out in front of himself and redirected Hayden's energy stream to a pile of debris next to his father. The resultant explosion of rubbish broke Hayden's concentration for a moment. Time sped up.

Hayden refocused and resumed the time freeze, observing that the tip of Amaris' sword was now only a couple inches away from Elle's side. Amaris continued his relentless assault and hit Hayden with a concentrated beam of energy head on.

Pain began to build in Hayden's body as he stood firm and attempted to withstand the blast while keeping time at a near-standstill. Worry began to cloud his mind as he felt his resolve slipping. The pain soon became unbearable.

As soon as Amaris felt Hayden's grip on time release, he ended his attack. Elle gasped for air and screamed as the blade sliced through her flesh and sunk deep into her side. Hayden watched helplessly as the tip of Amaris' sword emerged from Elle's abdomen, just below her left ribcage.

"Babe..." Elle screamed in a broken desperate plea, reaching her arm out toward Hayden.

Hayden staggered forward, smoke rising from his body. Pain radiated from every muscle with each step he took. As he neared Elle, he saw her blood pouring from the entrance and exit wounds made by Amaris' blade. It was running down her body and had begun to pool on the concrete below. Her breathing became ragged and labored as Hayden took her hand. Amaris withdrew the sword from her body and Elle fell to her knees.

"Now you know how I feel," Amaris said, a snide tone

of victory painting each word as they left his lips.

"Chantiatus," Hayden muttered in a flat despondent tone. A forcefield flickered to life around Elle and Kiera.

The already dull sky became pitch black, the only source of light now was the intense energy that was rolling off of Hayden's body in waves. Thunder echoed loudly through the desolate cityscape and lightning poured from the sky.

"It's over, I won," Amaris yelled. "Give it up and mourn with your wife in the few moments she has left."

The enormous shockwave of energy that emanated from Hayden's body sent Amaris sliding back on his heels several feet. The amulet flashed to life, the blinding orange light increasing in intensity until it appeared almost fiery red. In the distance, cars and buildings lit ablaze and the endless bolts of lightning intensified across the sky. Amaris attempted to attack Hayden, but it seemed to have no effect.

"Stop! You'll kill us all," Amaris yelled as he watched blocks of stone melt amongst the rubble of the building.

Hayden ignored him and let the rage take over. The ground began to violently shake and spasm. The wind that whipped through the landscape rose to a gale and then ignited. Around Hayden's body an immense bubble of catastrophic energy began to build.

"Let the world burn," Hayden said as he released the

shockwave of energy.

In an instant, the shockwave leveled everything in its path for dozens of miles, setting the air on fire and vaporizing anything in its way. The diameter of the shockwave continued to grow with no apparent reduction in its speed or devastating effect. The forcefield around Elle and Kiera began to flicker in impending failure under the relentless pressure. The field that Amaris had brought up to protect himself was suffering the same fate. In a few seconds, the shockwave would complete its extinction-inducing journey around the globe. Amaris panicked in the face of his coming death as his forcefield started to fail and pieces of his flesh began to tear away from the bone. In one last desperate attempt, he reached his hand out toward Hayden.

"Chronish'balseivius Parov," Amaris yelled just before his vocal cords began to burn away.

The flash of pure white light was blinding. Hayden flew backwards and felt as if his body was being ripped from the seams. Amaris opened his eyes to see that Hayden was gone.

"It may have worked," he thought to himself just before the forcefields surrounding himself, Elle, and Kiera gave way. He watched the two girls turn to dust just before he blacked out and his body was vaporized as well.

ↁ ↁ ↁ ↁ ↁ ↁ

Hayden opened his eyes and immediately noticed that the pain that had been overwhelming his body just moments ago was gone. He looked at his surroundings and felt a chill run through his body at the recognition of where he was.

"I must be dead," he thought to himself.

As he walked around the familiar living room of the Hensley's home in Camarillo, he noted that everything was in place exactly as he remembered it.

"This can't be real. This house was destroyed during the meteorite disaster in 2023," Hayden mumbled. He briefly pinched his forearm as a quasi-test to determine if he was dreaming. The momentary sharp pain led him to conclude that he was very much awake.

Hayden continued to look around and came upon the smart home hub that sat on the end table near the couch. He tapped on the screen and it woke up. Hayden stared at the screen in disbelief.

"June 7, 2020," Hayden said aloud to himself. "This is the past?"

Noting the relative quiet in the front of the house, Hayden wandered toward the dining room area. He froze as he saw a figure in the backyard through the glass panes on the french doors. Hayden looked closer and determined that the figure was Elle's older brother, Pete.

"Okay, yeah now this is getting weird," Hayden thought. "The last time I saw Pete he was dead."

Once Hayden figured out that Pete was more focused on diving into the swimming pool than anything going on inside the house, he cautiously proceeded to investigate further.

"Wait, if Pete is here..." Hayden thought, his memory now returned to the last few dire moments before he arrived in the house. "Then maybe Elle is here too."

Hayden felt a sudden rush of hope and anticipation surge through his body. The images of his recent fight with Amaris and the sword piercing through Elle's side were once again fresh in his mind. He felt a desperate desire to find Elle... if she was in the house. Hayden walked down the hallway toward Elle's bedroom. The door was cracked open and he heard the sound of music, accompanied by Elle's voice singing along to the lyrics. Hayden felt a pit in his stomach as he drew closer to the door.

Just before reaching Elle's room, a sudden feeling

overwhelmed Hayden's senses. It was the same feeling he had right after Amaris cast some spell that Hayden had never heard before. The feeling of being ripped apart at the seams. Hayden stopped in the hallway and focused his mind. The feeling passed and he stepped in front of Elle's bedroom door. Hayden took a deep breath, placed his palm against the door, and then pushed it open.

Elle sat on her bed, thumbing through a magazine and singing along to "Sink" by Noah Kahan. As the door opened she looked up and stopped singing.

"Hayden!" she said, her voice high-pitched with excitement. Elle jumped up off from her bed to greet him.

"Elle," Hayden replied, his voice quiet and contemplative.

"Are you okay?" Elle asked. "My parents went out shopping, so it's just me and Pete here right now."

"Yeah, I'm good. It's good to see you again," Hayden replied, trying to make sure his voice sounded normal and not fret with the feelings that were actually swirling around in his mind. "I was just passing through town and I thought I would swing by real quick to see if anyone was here. It's been a little while since I visited last."

"Like nine months. Just before you started going to college," Elle confirmed.

"Right," Hayden agreed then momentarily lost his words as he stared at Elle. A flash of thoughts rushed through his mind, like the feelings of deja vu he got when an Ane'illuminus inspired dream was about to come true. He knew that he had never dreamed about these moments, but he couldn't quite put his finger on why everything felt so familiar.

As one feeling subsided, another one came roaring back. The feeling that he was being ripped out of existence. Hayden fought it, but it persisted. He concluded that soon he would probably disappear and wind up in some other place, in some other time.

"Elle, I have to get going," Hayden said. "It was really great to see you."

"I wish you could stay longer," Elle replied.

"I know, me too," Hayden agreed. "Believe me, there's nothing I'd like more than to spend the rest of the day here. Nowadays, I always feel like I'm running out of time. One day though, everything will be okay. You just keep being you."

"I'll see you later," Elle said as Hayden walked toward the door.

Hayden paused at the door for a moment and then looked back at Elle. The feeling in his body of impending disappearance was growing stronger. He walked back over to her bedside and stood in front of her. Hayden took a deep breath, realizing that this may be the last time he would ever see Elle, and then placed his hand on her cheek.

"I love you, Elle," Hayden said softly.

Elle looked into Hayden's eyes, not entirely sure what to say. After a brief moment, Hayden turned and walked back to the door. Elle smiled at him and waved. He closed the door behind himself and started walking back down the hallway toward the front room. Three steps into the journey, Hayden vanished into thin air.

غير

Chapter Eight

Paradox

A warm breeze brushed along Hayden's cheek as he appeared, standing on the sidewalk in front of a schoolyard. He instantly knew where he was. This was his old elementary school in Moorpark.

"Okay, so *when* am I?" Hayden asked himself.

He looked around for clues. No newspapers in sight, no random clock showing the date. His phone and watch were frozen on the date and time he left 2024 with Kiera. A buzzer rang in the distance from the school building. Moments later, a stampede of children emerged from the building and into the schoolyard. Hayden peered through the steel fence to see if he recognized anyone or anything.

"Oh my God, it's me," Hayden muttered as he saw his younger self running across the grass toward the playground.

"I know exactly what day this is."

Hayden watched as his nine-year-old self stopped at the swingset and waited patiently for a kid to free up a swing. Two girls approached and stood behind him.

"You can cut in front of me if you want," young Hayden said to the girls. "I can wait if you two want to swing together."

"Thank you. That's really nice," the older girl said. "My name is Paige and this is my little sister Kali."

"I'm Hayden," he replied. "Are you in fifth grade also? You're not in my class."

"I am," Paige said. "I'm in Mrs. Lee's class. My sister is only eight years old, so she's not in our grade yet."

"Hey, all three of us can swing together," Paige said as she noticed a group of kids abandon their swings.

Hayden watched as his younger self spent the remainder of recess talking to and interacting with Paige and Kali. As the buzzer sounded announcing that classes were about to resume, Kali quietly wandered away as young Hayden and Paige talked to each other. She was making her way toward the fence on the edge of the schoolyard.

"You're not supposed to be here," eight-year-old Kali said to Hayden as she stood in front of him on the other side of the fence.

"What do you mean?" Hayden asked her.

"If you're here, then someone changed things," she replied.

"You know who I am?" Hayden asked.

"Yeah, you're him," Kali replied as she pointed back at the younger version of Hayden.

Hayden felt the unmistakable feeling of being ripped from the timeline overcoming his senses. Kali turned and ran back to accompany the others into the school and Hayden vanished.

❧ ❧ ❧ ❧ ❧ ❧

May 28, 2022 - Alternate Timeline

The scent of pine trees filled Hayden's nostrils as he reappeared. As he looked around the campground area, he recognized the location as Yosemite National Park. The sound of a zipper opening on a nearby tent drew his attention. Paige emerged from the tent and walked over to the picnic table to retrieve a bottled water from the ice chest.

"This must be Paige's camping trip with her family back in 2022," Hayden thought to himself. Hayden approached Paige cautiously as to not frighten her.

"Hey Paige," he said as he walked up to her. "It's good to see you."

Paige continued to sift through the ice water in search of a beverage as if she didn't hear him.

"Paige!" Hayden repeated in a raised voice.

No response. Paige cracked open a bottle and began drinking some water. She was now facing Hayden, but made no indication that she could see him.

"Why can't she see or hear me?" he asked himself. "Elle could see me when I flashed into that moment in time. Little Kali could see me at the schoolyard. What is different about this time?"

"Hayden!" Paige called out, as she looked back over her shoulder.

"Be out there in a sec," a voice replied from another tent.

"Okay, this is weird," Hayden thought. "This is not what actually happened. I stayed back in Fullerton when Paige went on this trip."

Moments later, Hayden watched as another version of himself emerged from the second tent. Now he was certain that his must be some kind of alternate timeline. No one seemed to be able to see or hear him. Hayden decided to just watch and see how things played out in this version of history.

"Is your phone working?" Paige asked Hayden as she handed him a plate of hashbrowns and eggs that her father had left for them before going on a morning hike with her mother.

"Nope," he replied in between bites of food. "I woke up at like four o'clock and it had no signal then either."

"Oh well," Paige replied. "Who needs them when you're out in such a beautiful place. I'm just glad that I was able to talk you into coming with us on this trip."

"Me too," Hayden said. "It does feel good to get out of Fullerton and relax outdoors for a change. I can't believe I was going to stay home and study instead of doing this."

"So are you ready for a fun-filled day of hiking and campfires?" Paige asked. "We're going to... what is that? Is there a fire?"

Hayden looked back over his shoulder in the direction Paige was pointing. Two large clouds rose in the distance to the west and northwest. Moments later, two more clouds became visible in the southern and southeastern skies.

"That's not a fire," Hayden said, his voice flat and serious. He stood and raised his hand in the air for a few moments. "Wind is blowing northeast, we should be okay here."

"Okay from what?" Paige asked, the concern now

evident in her voice after Hayden's behavior.

"Fallout," he replied. "Those were nuclear blasts, I'm sure of it."

"What?!" Paige exclaimed, the concern now turning into fear. "You mean someone dropped nuclear bombs?"

"Yeah, I'm guessing based on the directions of those clouds they hit Sacramento, San Francisco, Las Vegas, and somewhere in the central valley, maybe Bakersfield."

"What about Fullerton?" Paige asked, fearing she knew the answer.

"We wouldn't be able to see anything from here, but I'd imagine that Los Angeles was hit," Hayden replied. "Most likely somewhere in Orange County also."

"What are we going to do?" Paige asked.

"Right now, we should…" Hayden began, but his sentence was cut short as he collapsed onto the ground.

"Hayden!" Paige screamed as she rushed over to his side and attempted to wake him.

Despite Paige's efforts, Hayden lay unconscious for several minutes. She could tell that he was breathing and had a pulse, so her immediate panic subsided somewhat. Eventually, Paige noticed what seemed to be an aura of faint white light hovering over Hayden's body that appeared to settle into his chest.

"...look for some shelter," Hayden finished his sentence as he woke and then gasped for air.

"What happened?" Paige asked. "You fainted and were unconscious for like five minutes."

"I don't know," Hayden admitted. "I feel different."

Hayden closed his eyes and concentrated for a few moments. Paige studied his face, hoping to glean some information from his mannerisms.

"This is going to sound crazy," Hayden said. "But I think that I can *do things*."

"What do you mean by do things?" Paige asked.

Hayden stepped over to the edge of the picnic table area and held his hand out in front of him. A symbol began to illuminate on the back of his hand. A crackle of electricity formed in his palm and shot straight out toward a nearby boulder.

"What was that?!" Paige screamed.

"There's more," Hayden replied as he felt a rush of power in his body and a sudden influx of knowledge. "The bombs... Wait, where is Kali at right now?"

"She's in Washington still, at her college," Paige replied.

"I'll be back," Hayden said. His feet left the ground and he levitated above it for a few moments before taking off in flight and vanishing into the horizon.

ↂ ↂ ↂ ↂ ↂ ↂ

Hayden arrived in Washington and burst into the front door of Kali's dorm, frantically searching for her. He noticed that the television was on in the living room and ingredients for a sandwich were still out on the kitchen counter.

"Kali, are you in here?" Hayden yelled.

"Hayden?" Kali asked as she peeked her head out of her bedroom door.

"Come on, we have to go," Hayden demanded as he ran down the hall and took her by the hand.

"Wait, what are you doing? What are you talking about?" Kali asked assertively. "You're scaring me."

"Be scared," Hayden replied. "Something horrible is about to happen."

Kali relented and ran with Hayden out of the residence hall to the courtyard. He wrapped one of his arms around her torso and told her to hold on to him. After a moment of hesitation, she acquiesced. Hayden rose from the ground and Kali grasped him tighter in fear from the sudden and unexplained occurrence.

Hayden pulled Kali's face into his shoulder as a bright

flash of light pulsed in the northern sky, about thirty miles away. He took flight back toward Yosemite with immense speed. Kali peeked back over Hayden's shoulder and watched as the mushroom cloud rose above the city she had just been in a few seconds prior.

About thirty minutes later, Hayden set down in the campground at Yosemite. Paige came running up to him and Kali.

"Paige!" Kali yelled as she met her sister in a hug. "Hayden got us out of the city just as the blast was going off. One more minute and I would've probably been dead."

"Thank you, Hayden," Paige mouthed as she continued the embrace with Kali.

"Yeah, thank you," Kali said as he turned back to Hayden. "I don't even know how I could ever repay you."

"I'm just glad you're safe," Hayden replied. "That's enough."

"So sweet," Paige joked.

Kali and Hayden exchanged glances. Paige's comment flared the awkwardness of their relationship back to life. They hadn't spoken to each other in some time after Kali abruptly left Southern California.

"Yeah, it was," Kali finally concurred. "I left. I'm sorry, I was wrong. I realize that now… I've been slowly realizing it for a while. If you don't hate me, then I'd like to talk to you about it, Hayden."

"Hate you?" Hayden replied. "Of course I don't hate you. Let's talk this evening after we've found some shelter and have settled in."

"Okay, I'd like that," Kali said, a faint smile returning to her face.

"Alright, for now let's pack up some stuff and move," Hayden said. "Grab any canned or sealed foods, bottled water, and our backpacks or suitcases. Leave anything that's opened already or exposed to the air, just to be safe. I had a look around while Kali and I were flying here. It looks like all of the blasts are a considerable distance from here and wind is driving the fallout plumes in other directions. We should be safe just bunkering up in a cabin for now until we figure out our next moves."

"I'm going to leave a note for my parents here on the picnic table and let them know which direction we are heading. I hope they can find us," Paige said. "Maybe in the morning we can go out and search for them?"

"Yeah, of course we can," Hayden replied. "Knowing your father, they probably found a cave and are trying to wait it out until he thinks it's safe. So even if we don't find them tomorrow, I'm sure that they will make their way to us. They

___

will find the notes we've left and find us."

ᔕ ᔕ ᔕ ᔕ ᔕ ᔕ

Later that night, after the trio had sealed the cabin as well as they could from outside air, they decided to try and get some rest. Paige headed to one of the bedrooms and quickly fell asleep. Kali joined Hayden in another bedroom to have the discussion that they had postponed earlier.

"So, I've been thinking about you a lot recently," Kali started as she sat on the bed next to Hayden. "I made a mistake by leaving. I was planning on coming back to Orange County after the semester ended and surprising you."

"Really?" Hayden asked. "That definitely would have been a surprise. Maybe *shock* is a better word, actually."

"I know it all sounds so stupid," Kali continued. "Just showing up out of nowhere and expecting that you'd welcome me after I just took off… expecting that you hadn't already moved on, with someone else."

"I'm single, Kali," Hayden replied. "I guess you could say that I never really moved on."

"You saved my life today," Kali said, half under her breath as if she were still processing the fact. "If you hadn't thought about me then I would have been killed in that blast."

"You say that like me forgetting about you is an actual possibility," Hayden replied sarcastically.

Kali didn't respond. Instead she stared into Hayden's eyes for several seconds before giving in to her impulses, leaning in, and kissing Hayden on the lips.

"Now that's a good way to say thank you," Hayden joked as the kiss ended.

"Shut up," Kali replied as she stood up and removed her shirt and pajama pants. "Just shut up and take your clothes off."

Hayden complied with Kali's request as quickly as he could. Anticipatory silence filled the room as Kali climbed back into the bed on top of Hayden.

Ↄ Ↄ Ↄ Ↄ Ↄ Ↄ

May 29, 2022 - 2:30 a.m. - Alternate Timeline

The creak of the wooden window shutters in the breeze woke Hayden. He looked over to see Kali cuddled up next to him. After carefully climbing out of the bed, Hayden slipped on a pair of shorts and walked down to the living room of the cabin. He wasn't sure if it was the sound of the shutters or the uneasy feeling that was washing over his mind that had actually woke him up.

As he sat down on the plain-looking couch, Hayden heard a voice calling out. It was distant and seemed to be in his mind.

"Now I'm going crazy," he thought to himself. The voice continued.

"My name is Armond el-Hashem," the voice said. "I am reaching out to all four of you telepathically at the same time. No doubt, by now, you have all discovered that you received certain special abilities or powers yesterday after the global nuclear war began. There is an enormous threat coming very soon that has the potential to end all life on the planet, even more of a threat than the bombs that were dropped. I need you all to listen and do as I say if we hope to save humanity."

Hayden continued to listen to the voice as Armond explained about the Alva'ci, the creature's imminent emergence, the existence of the ancient powers and the prophecies. Armond told Hayden and the others that he was trapped deep underground in the subway system of New York City to avoid nuclear fallout. Finally, Armond instructed everyone that they needed to meet up, that day, in Yosemite prepared to fight the Alva'ci.

As the voice finished speaking, Hayden felt a sense

of normalcy return to his mind. He stood up to return to bed, but stumbled and fell back on to the couch as a jolting tremor shook throughout the region. He regained his composure and ran down the hallway to check on Kali and Paige.

"Are you guys okay?" Hayden asked as the sisters emerged from each bedroom.

"Yeah, I'm okay," Paige confirmed, while looking her sister up and down as she noticed that she was only dressed in a thin white sheet that she had hastily grabbed from the bed. "Looks like Kali is doing pretty good too."

"Uhh, yeah, I'm all good," Kali said, knowing that Paige had already added up what her and Hayden had been up to earlier in the night.

"Let's all try to get some more sleep," Hayden said. "I have a feeling that tomorrow is going to be very busy."

℘ ℘ ℘ ℘ ℘ ℘

May 29, 2022 - 9:30 a.m. - Alternate Timeline

Paige sat down at the dining room table and joined Kali and Hayden. They began an unorthodox breakfast of various canned goods. As they ate, a knock on the front door of the cabin startled them.

"I'll check it out," Hayden said as he rose from his chair and cautiously approached the front door.

"Hayden de Vere?" a voice called from the other side of the door. "That voice… Armond sent us here to meet you. My name is Mackenzie. I'm here with Tiffany and Shaun."

Hayden opened the door and saw Mackenzie and her two companions. He welcomed them inside and began explaining to Kali and Paige what he had experienced in the middle of the night.

"So, a bunch of nukes get dropped and wipe out cities full of people, including six other people that are like the four of you," Kali began. "…and because of that, some evil alien lifeform is going to attack and wipe out everything that's left?"

"Pretty much," Mackenzie confirmed. "Unless we can stop it, that is."

Another earthquake shook the cabin, this one stronger than the last. Even after the major shaking subsided, a constant light tremor continued to run through the ground.

"I want to go with you," Kali said to Hayden.

"It's not safe," Hayden told her.

"I'll stay out of the way," she replied. "If this thing is going to wipe out the planet, then I want my last moments to be around you, not hiding out in some cabin waiting to die."

As the earthquake picked up intensity again, a thundering boom echoed through the valley. The group ran outside and saw a pillar of smoke rising from the area a half-mile north of them. They sprinted toward the clearing and found the source. A crater pocked the earth and billowed dark smoke from it's center.

"Stay right here," Hayden instructed Kali and Paige.

Hayden led Mackenzie, Tiffany, and Shaun closer to the edge of the crater. A bright orange flash stunned them momentarily. Out of the smoke, the Alva'ci walked toward them. Shaun took the initiative and rushed toward the Alva'ci, activating his powers as he ran. The creature deflected Shaun's attack with ease and fired off a counterattack that hit Shaun square in the chest, causing massive damage. He died before his body hit the ground.

"Oh my God," Tiffany stuttered in a panicked voice. "It killed him just like that."

"We have to be smart about this," Hayden said. "Just follow my…"

Before Hayden could finish his sentence, the Alva'ci fired off two enormous streams of energy at Tiffany and Mackenzie, vaporizing them both instantly.

"Shit," Hayden mumbled, realizing that he may be in over his head.

The Alva'ci poised itself for another attack. Hayden focused and felt the powers of Shaun, Mackenzie, and Tiffany enter his body. He opened his eyes to see the Alva'ci beginning to attack. Hayden concentrated and deflected the attack into the mountainside, sending rock and dust hundreds of feet into the air. Hayden summoned all he knew of his powers and cast them all at once at the creature, who was not expecting a counterattack. The blow landed and broke away fragments of the creature's armor.

"You must be the cognizant one," the Alva'ci said. "It figures that you're the only one capable enough to last more than one blow with me."

Hayden and the Alva'ci went back and forth for several minutes, attacking each other. A tiny sliver of hope returned in Hayden's mind. Perhaps he actually had a chance at winning.

Growing impatient, the Alva'ci scanned the edge of the clearing and spotted Paige and Kali. In another bright flash of orange light, the creature teleported away from the battlefield and reappeared behind the girls. Paige attempted to run, but the Alva'ci backhanded her and sent her flying several yards. Paige landed in the dust, unconscious.

Kali was frozen in place with fear. Hayden rose from the ground and flew over to the edge of the clearing to confront the Alva'ci. As he landed, the creature grabbed Kali by the back of the neck and drew her in close.

"Let her go!" Hayden shouted. "Those two don't even have powers. Fight me."

"They'll all be dead soon anyway," the Alva'ci mocked. "This will be a lot quicker than what the rest of humanity gets."

Hayden watched as the armor around the creature's fist changed shape into a sharp knife-like appendage. It thrust the sharp blade into Kali's back and out her chest. Kali screamed in horrifying pain and passed out as the creature withdrew the blade. As the Alva'ci was about to toss Kali's body aside, a purple light began to emanate from her chest. The light grew brighter and swirled around her body. Kali regained consciousness and the wound appeared to have healed.

"What power is this?" the Alva'ci said. "It couldn't be."

While the creature was distracted by Kali's miraculous recovery, Hayden saw a moment of opportunity. He sprinted toward the Alva'ci and produced a blade of pure white energy. He drove the blade into the neck of the Alva'ci and pulled it sideways. The creature's head fell to the ground, its body collapsing seconds later. Hayden took Kali in his arms and held her.

"What happened there?" Hayden asked.

"I don't know," Kali admitted.

As Paige regained consciousness and sat up, the body of the Alva'ci began to disintegrate and form into a ball of intensely glowing orange light. The orb-like shape of energy exploded and hit Hayden and Kali head on.

"I feel so much stronger," Hayden said as he absorbed the energy. "We should all go back to the cabin and recover."

"It's too much," Kali screamed as she buried her head in her hands.

Hayden attempted to comfort her, but Kali broke away from his embrace and stood up.

"Kali, let's go rest. We all need it," Hayden said as he started to walk over to her.

"I have work to finish," Kali replied in a cold, flat voice before teleporting away.

༄ ༄ ༄ ༄ ༄ ༄

May 29, 2022 - 11:30 a.m. - Alternate Timeline

Paige sat on the couch in the cabin, staring out the window and lost in thought. Hayden paced around the living room trying to figure out what had just occurred.

"Where did my sister go?" Paige asked. "How did she do that?"

"I don't know," Hayden answered. "What she said before she left, that didn't sound like her. Something bad happened to her. We'll figure it all out and get her back."

"Have you talked to your parents at all, Hayden?" Paige asked. "You know, since all of the bombs dropped and everything?"

"No," Hayden said as he sighed. "I know I need to see if they're okay, but at the same time I'm scared to know. My father had a conference this week, so they're out of town. Will you be okay here if I go to check on them? Or do you want to come with me?"

"I want to come with you," Paige replied. "I don't want to be here alone."

"Okay, let's go," Hayden said. "You should leave a note here, in case your parents find the cabin."

"Good idea," Paige said and wrote out a quick letter.

ഗ ഗ ഗ ഗ ഗ ഗ

May 29, 2022 - 12:15 p.m. - Alternate Timeline

Hayden and Paige touched down outside his parents' hotel in Flagstaff, Arizona. The town was eerily quiet. As they walked inside, they found the front desk abandoned. Hayden leapt the counter and looked through the paperwork sprawled out on the floor.

"Room 323," he said.

Paige and Hayden arrived at the room and knocked on the door. They heard a brief shuffling around in the room and then moments later the door opened.

"Hayden!" his mother cried and hugged him. "Oh, Paige, you're here too! I'm so glad you're both safe."

"We're glad you guys are safe too," Paige replied as Hayden's father rounded the corner and joined them.

"I've been trying to call the Hensley's since yesterday, but the phones are all down," Annie said. "They were on a cruise up to Alaska."

"Well, if they were still on the ship, then maybe they were safe from the bombs," Hayden replied.

"I hope so," Annie said. "I wish there was some way to know."

"I can check on them," Hayden told her.

"How would you do that?" Annie asked. "Wait, how are you two here? I thought you guys were in Yosemite this weekend."

"It's a long story," Hayden replied. "I'll fill you in later, but if you want me to check on the Hensley's then I should go now."

"Okay, but be careful," Annie said.

"Are you okay to stay here with my parents?" Hayden asked Paige.

"Of course," she replied.

"I'll be back as soon as I can, don't leave the hotel."

೮೨ ೮೨ ೮೨ ೮೨ ೮೨ ೮೨

May 29, 2022 - 2:30 p.m. - Alternate Timeline
Juneau, Alaska

Hayden arrived to find the city bustling with activity. People were in a panic trying to find food and news of what was happening in the rest of the world. By a stroke of luck, Hayden spotted Elle Hensley in a crowd of people near a convenience store. He ran over to her family.

"You're all okay?" Hayden asked as he approached.

"Hayden!" Elle screamed as she noticed him, then gripped him tightly in a hug.

"We're okay," Gabe said. "They're saying that Anchorage got hit with a nuke. Edmonton and Vancouver also."

"Yeah, lots of places got hit," Hayden confirmed.

"What are we going to do?" Elle asked, the glee in her

voice now turning back to the fear that had been gripping her mind before.

"My parents and my friend Paige are bunkered down in a hotel in Flagstaff," Hayden said. "If we head back there, then we can all figure out what to do together."

"That's a long ways away," Gabe said.

"Next in line!" a male voice yelled from the door of the convenience store.

"That's us," Gabe said. "We're going to buy some food and water and then we can discuss things more."

Gabe, Martha, and Pete walked into the convenience store. The owner had set up a barricade at the front entrance and was only letting one family in at a time to try and prevent looting. Elle stayed outside with Hayden.

"Thank you for checking on us," Elle said as they strolled down the sidewalk together.

"Of course," Hayden replied. "How are you doing?"

"I'm scared," she admitted. "Everyone here is panicking and I'm not sure it's going to be safe in this town for much longer."

"Well, I'm not going to let anyone hurt you," Hayden said. "So, banish that thought from your mind."

Elle smiled as she felt a little relief with Hayden's words. "Thank you."

Just as Elle's family walked out of the convenience store, the sky grew noticeably darker. A faint glimmer of orange light appeared in the now otherwise blackened sky.

"Oh my God, it's a bomb!" a woman's voice screamed in the distance as she pointed to the sky.

The orange glow intensified and Hayden realized that it was not a nuclear bomb. He braced himself mentally for a possible fight.

As Kali appeared in the sky, the crowds of people panicked. Some took shelter in the nearby shops, some ran, and others stood frozen at the spectacle. Kali descended and levitated about twenty feet above Hayden.

"I am going to need the rest of that power you absorbed from the Alva'ci," she shouted at Hayden.

"You don't seem well," Hayden replied. "Come here and let me figure out what's wrong with you."

"There's nothing wrong with me," she answered. "I am exceptional. I am extraordinary. I am all-powerful. Or I will be as soon as I have your powers."

"You're starting to sound crazy," Hayden said. "Besides, I can't just give you my powers."

"That is true," Kali replied. "Unfortunately, you're going to have to die."

Kali pointed the palm of her right hand at a nearby

mountain. As her hand began to glow fiercely with an orange light, the ground shook and the face of the mountain started to crumble. Elle positioned herself behind Hayden in fear.

A thunderous clap roared across the town as several thousand tons of rock separated from the rest of the mountain and floated in the air near Kali. Most of the citizens that were still watching the scene unfold began to run for cover. Gabe and the rest of Elle's family ran toward Hayden and Elle.

"Goodbye Hayden," Kali said as she thrust her palm forward toward the town. The enormous ball of rock hurtled toward the street.

"Chantiatus," Hayden yelled.

A forcefield flickered into existence around Hayden and Elle just as the deadly avalanche of stone hit the city, destroying everything and killing everyone.

Elle opened her eyes, expecting to be dead. Instead she saw Hayden still standing in front of her and a weird glowing field around them. As the dust settled, she saw that nothing else was left.

"They're gone," she stuttered. "My parents and my brother… they were just right there, almost to us… and now they're gone. They're dead."

"I've got you, Elle," was all that Hayden could say in

the moment. He pulled her in close with his right arm and then used his left hand to fire off a staggering blast of energy at Kali, who teleported away before the attack could hit her.

Elle broke down and sobbed into Hayden's shoulder. He continued to hold her as he looked around the barren wasteland that had just been a city. Elle was correct, there was absolutely nothing left for miles in every direction.

"Hold on to me," Hayden told Elle. "We're going to Flagstaff."

❧ ❧ ❧ ❧ ❧ ❧

Late June 2022 - Alternate Timeline
Somewhere in Montana

After another time jump, Hayden appeared outside a group of cabins in a decidedly rural area. He proceeded inside the closest cabin and found that once again no one present could see or hear him. He continued to watch the events of this alternate history unfold.

His alternate self sat at the kitchen table, studying a map of the United States of America. It was thoroughly marked up with notes and circles around various cities.

"I'm going to take a break for a week or so," Hayden

said to Elle, who was in the kitchen.

"Good. You need to take a break," Elle replied as she flipped a pancake on the stove. "I know you want to save everything you can and I think that's amazing and wonderful, but you need to look out for yourself too. Plus, I need you here. Everyone else has been great and supportive, but I just feel so much safer when you're here with us."

"I will start taking shorter trips after the break," Hayden concurred. "Using these powers to neutralize the nuclear fallout takes a lot out of me.

"I know it does," Elle said. "You need some time to relax and enjoy what we've built here. We actually have electricity, landlines, and hot showers. You, Dan, and your dad did a really good job of making this place safe and livable."

"Did you ever think you'd be reliant on a landline phone?" Hayden joked.

"Never," Elle replied as she laughed. "But it beats walking to the other cabins when I need to say something quick."

A knock on the front door interrupted the conversation. Before Hayden could get up to open the door, Dan peered through the window and yelled his name. Paige stood next to him shaking her head and laughing.

ω ω ω ω ω ω

February 2023 - Alternate Timeline
Southwestern Florida

The next time flash took Hayden to somewhere he was wholly unfamiliar with. Kali was lying at the end of a twin-size bed and groaning in pain. A small gathering of her followers were assembled in the room.

"Okay, let's push again," the young woman positioned in between Kali's legs said. "The baby is almost here. Just one more good push."

Hayden watched as Kali gave birth and the young woman placed the baby on her chest. Kali breathed in a deep sigh of relief.

"His name will be Amaris," Kali told the young woman. "I must embark on a mission to find the source of my powers. As my followers, I entrust my baby to you. I have no interest in raising a child. Protect him until he is old enough to travel and then take him to his father's settlement. Leave him there. I do not need him tagging along and hindering your preparations for longer than necessary."

"Where is his father?" the young woman asked.

"Last I knew, he was in Montana. I will circle the

area on your map," Kali replied. "His name is Hayden de Vere. I advise you not to engage with him. Just drop the child outside the city walls where he can easily be found."

"We will do as you wish."

"I may not return for a long time, perhaps a dozen years," Kali said. "When I come back, be ready. I will destroy our enemies, make this world mine, and then retrieve the child to serve at my side. You will live in paradise."

"Yes, Kali. We will be ready," several people in the room chanted in unison.

ℕ ℕ ℕ ℕ ℕ ℕ

April 2026 - Alternate Timeline
Montana Settlement

Hayden arrived back in the rural Montana landscape. The small grouping of cabins had grown into an almost small town of sorts. Another dozen cabins stood nearby, along with several ancillary buildings. Men, women, and children that Hayden had never seen before moved throughout the settlement.

"This must be at least a few years in the future from the last time I saw this place," Hayden thought to himself.

He walked over to the same cabin that he had visited last time and entered to see what events unfolded. As he walked inside, he noticed a makeshift calendar hanging on the wall and concluded that it was sometime in April 2026.

Abby and Elle sat on the living room couch and were whispering to each other. Alternate timeline Hayden walked down the hallway and into the living room to join Elle and Abby.

"So, Elle has something to tell you," Abby teased, her voice suspiciously giddy.

"Okay…" Hayden replied, obviously intrigued. "What's up?"

"Show him," Abby whispered to Elle as she nudged her with an elbow.

Elle slowly rose from the couch and walked over to the chair that Hayden was sitting in. She held out her closed fist and then slowly opened it. Hayden took the object from her hand and examined it closely.

"Really?" Hayden asked, his voice now rife with excitement.

"Yep," Elle confirmed as she shook her head. "That's the third one I've taken today. Just wanted to be super sure."

"We're having a baby," Hayden said as he stood and hugged Elle. "That's incredible."

______

PARADOX

⁍ ⁍ ⁍ ⁍ ⁍ ⁍

June 1, 2022 - Alternate Timeline
New York City

Hayden's head pounded as he appeared from the time jump into the dark confines of a subway tunnel maintenance room. He regained his composure and looked around. In the corner of the room sat Armond, hunched over a book in the dim light of a candle.

As Armond thumbed through the pages of the book, he underlined passages that he deemed important and wrote notes in the margins. Hayden approached and looked over Armond's shoulder. He immediately recognized the book as the one that Amaris had stolen from Armond, Powers and Practices.

"Maybe I can see something here that will help me stop these time flashes," Hayden thought as he continued to read over Armond's shoulder.

Once Armond reached the end of the book, he placed it on top of several others and tucked them all into a small crevice in the brick wall. Armond fiddled with his coat pocket and withdrew a rag. As he drew it to his face, Armond let out a long hacking cough. Hayden noticed that the rag was covered in blood as Armond placed it back in his pocket.

"Oh man, the fallout here must be getting to him," Hayden thought.

"Okay, Armond," he said aloud to himself. "You're work is almost done."

Hayden concentrated on one of the many spells that he had learned from reading over Armond's shoulder. As he felt the next time jump approaching, Hayden opened a portal, chanted the spell, and leapt inside.

ക്ക ക്ക ക്ക ക്ക ക്ക ക്ക

56,000 BC - Standard Timeline
Prehistoric Mesopotamia

Hayden's portal opened, with the mixture of orange and purple light flooding the dark skies outside a small village. He tumbled out into the dirt and then rose to his feet.

A woman emerged from one of the small buildings and walked toward Hayden. She was attractive, perhaps late-20's, and her posture exuded confidence. She stopped in front of Hayden and examined him from head to toe.

"You are?" she asked.

"My name is Hayden de Vere," he replied.

"You have powers," she said. "However, you're not from the village."

"I am not," Hayden confirmed. "I am from the future. I was thrown into a series of time jumps by a spell. I just escaped it and came here to learn how to get back and make things right."

"I see," the woman said. "Do you know who I am?"

"I assume that you are Bilv'at," Hayden said.

"That is correct," she confirmed. "Come into my home and we will talk."

Hayden accompanied Bilv'at into the dwelling. The room was simple, lightly decorated with functional items, and the air filled with a sweet aroma.

"Give me you hand," Bilv'at instructed. "Let me examine your timeline."

Hayden held out his hand. Bilv'at took it in her hand and closed her eyes. Her eyelids danced around as if she were dreaming intensely. After a minute, she opened her eyes and released Hayden's hand.

"Quite the story," Bilv'at said. "You are quite a remarkable man. There has never been a man that could wield the powers over time, but you are able to. I will teach you what you need to know."

"Thank you," Hayden replied. "So many things went

wrong. I need to get back to a specific point in time and fix everything."

"You will be able to do so," Bilv'at said.

Hayden spent the next several hours learning various spells. Bilv'at held out her arms and an aura of purple light surrounded Hayden before settling in on his skin and disappearing.

"You will now be able to use your portals to travel through time instantly," Bilv'at said. "There will be no lag in time as with the method you used previously. Think of the exact moment in time you wish to travel to when you step into the portal and you will arrive there."

"Thank you," Hayden said.

"You're quite welcome," Bilv'at replied. "I am very pleased to have met you. Use the other spells that I taught you with extreme care. Some of those spells' benefits are things that you may only wish to share with those you love most. You are extremely intelligent and caring, I believe that you will do the right thing."

"I understand," Hayden replied. "You have my word that I will exercise caution."

"One last thing before you go," Bilv'at added. "The powers of the Princess of Time, the Amira al-Dahr... those powers are meant to be bestowed upon a female. As a sign of my faith in you, I grant you the ability to choose whichever girl or woman that you believe deserves the honor of the title and the breadth of that power. Once you have corrected your timeline and fixed your errors you may make a choice. Take your time, choose wisely."

Hayden nodded his head in agreement and opened a portal. The walls of the dwelling shimmered in the reflection of the bright purple field. Hayden concentrated on a moment in time and stepped into the light.

مستقر

Chapter Nine

Ahwahnee

2049 - Standard Timeline - Amaris' Base of Operations

The portal flashed open with a brilliant display of purple light. As Hayden stepped out, he experienced the same feeling that had occurred during the time jumps. It felt as if his mind and body were being pulled from existence. In a blur of white light, his essence merged with his body in the current timeline. Time was still frozen in place.

Hayden felt a jarring sensation as he came back into the moment. It was as if he had just reentered his own body. The fight with Amaris was underway. Hayden had come back moments before his son's sword was to pierce through Elle's flesh.

"It's time to fix this," he thought.

Concentrating on one of the new spells he had learned from Bilv'at, Hayden kept time frozen in place. He walked over to Elle and touched her on the shoulder, waking her from the time freeze.

"Come on, let's get out of here," Hayden told her as they stepped away from Amaris.

Hayden knelt down and woke Kiera from the time freeze. "Time to go home."

"Oh, yeah, let's go," Kiera replied softly. "I'm sorry I wasn't more help. I don't know what happened to me."

"It's okay," Hayden insisted. "This was your first time out in a real battle. Things happen that we cannot predict. We will continue working on your abilities."

Hayden waved his hand and a portal emblazoned with purple light appeared. As he led Elle and Kiera inside the time freeze ceased and Amaris seethed in his defeat.

ᘍ ᘍ ᘍ ᘍ ᘍ ᘍ

October 2024
Fullerton, California

Jared flung the bedroom door open as he stormed after Abby. It smashed up against the wall, leaving a hole in the drywall

———

in the shape of a doorknob.

"So, what, are you cheating on me?" Jared yelled.

"No, I'm not cheating. Are you crazy?" Abby replied. "You're the one who randomly disappears and doesn't have his phone on for hours at a time."

"Oh, so now I'm the bad guy for wanting to hang out with some of my other friends?" Jared said. "You overreact to everything."

"Me? You just put a hole in the wall!"

"You were hiding who you were talking to," Jared said.

"I was texting Elle!" Abby yelled.

"You're so insecure and paranoid that it's actually funny," Jared snarled. "It's so pathetic."

"You're an ass," Abby snapped back.

"You're lucky to have me," Jared's voice turned deep and serious as he put his hand around Abby's throat and slammed her up against the wall. "You don't deserve me. Maybe I do need another girl to keep me company."

Abby attempted to speak, but Jared tightened his grip. He looked at her menacingly as he watched Abby choke and try to gasp for air. Once he felt like she was about to pass out, he released his grip and Abby fell to the floor. She clutched at her neck and sucked in oxygen as fast as she could.

"I'm going to the bar," Jared declared. "Clean yourself

up and fix your attitude before I get back."

Abby struggled back up to her feet as she heard the front door slam shut. She walked to the window and peered through the blinds to see Jared's car speeding off down the street. Turning back to the bedroom, Abby wiped the tears from her eyes that had involuntarily welled up from being choked. She noticed that her entire body was sore from the impact against the wall as she struggled to the bathroom to look at her neck.

"Oh great," she mumbled as she noticed that the mirror that was hanging on the back of the bathroom door had shattered when Jared was throwing open various doors looking for her. The shards of glass littered the floor in front of the counter. She carefully stepped around the glass and looked at her neck in the mirror above the sink. A deep red bruise stretched across the tender skin that Jared had gripped with frightening force.

Returning to her bedroom, Abby remembered that she needed to text Elle back. She grabbed her phone from the bed and typed. "Sorry, Jared and I just had a big fight." She plugged her phone into the charger and walked down the hallway to the living room to observe the damage there.

"Maybe he's right," Abby thought to herself. "The first relationship I've been in for a long time and I can't even make things work."

Thirty minutes later, Abby found herself back in the bathroom. Her thoughts had spiraled from doubt to self-loathing. A heavy cloud of depression set in over her mind. She was beginning to slip back into the type of destructive thoughts that she had when she started attending college. In the background, she hardly noticed the chime of her phone's notifications ringing in the bedroom.

"Look at yourself," Abby said aloud as she stared in the mirror. "Just like always, you drive every guy in your life away. I hate what I see. Maybe this is what I deserve. Maybe he can just go find someone better than me."

Abby stripped her clothes off and carelessly tossed them in corner as the bathwater ran. She stepped into the hot water and then sunk down, immersing her nude body in the soothing heat. Abby breathed out a deep sigh of relief as she let her cares sink away into the water. From her bedroom, the faint sound of her phone ringing could be heard.

"Okay," she said to herself as she picked up the shard of mirror glass that she had set on the edge of the bathtub. Abby flinched and gasped as the jagged glass pierced the skin on her wrist. She took a moment to compose herself and work up the courage to continue, then pulled the glass down along her arm, cutting deep. Blood poured from her arm into the bathwater. She took the glass in her other hand and repeated the process on her other arm. As she watched the blood spill from her arm into the bath, she noticed the edges of her vision blurring and vignetting into darkness. Her body sunk forward into the water as she lost consciousness.

"Abby?" Elle called out from the threshold of the front door. "Are you in here? I've been trying to call you."

Elle walked around the living room. Her concern grew as she saw the disarray of the apartment. She dialed Abby's phone number again and heard it ring from down the hallway.

"Is she asleep or something?" Elle wondered as she walked down the hallway.

Light peeking through the cracked bathroom door drew Elle's attention. "Are you in there Abby?"

When there was no response, Elle pushed the bathroom door open. As broken glass crackled under her shoes, Elle saw why Abby hadn't been answering the phone. She immediately called Hayden.

"Come to Abby's right now, I need you," she said in a panic as Hayden answered his phone.

Behind Elle, a bright flash of orange appeared as Hayden stepped out of a portal. He immediately sprang into action as he saw the scene before him. Hayden scooped

Abby's body from the bath and placed her on the carpet in her bedroom.

"No pulse," he said as he felt Abby's neck. He moved his hand over her sternum and focused his powers. "Her heart muscles are quivering, she's in VFib."

"What do we do?" Elle asked.

"Grab some towels to wrap the wounds on her arms," Hayden instructed. "I'm going to shock her."

Hayden placed a hand on the right side of her chest below the collarbone and his other hand below her left breast cupping the edge of her chest. The symbol of Electricity began to glow on the back of his hands and Abby's body spasmed as a wave of electric current passed through it.

"Okay, wrap her arms now while I do CPR," Hayden told Elle.

After two minutes, Elle had finished bandaging the wounds and Hayden shocked Abby again. They watched for a moment in anticipation. Abby gasped for breath and opened her eyes. She groaned in intense pain and had a worried look on her face as she realized that Elle and Hayden had found her in the bathtub.

"What the hell, Abby?" Hayden muttered.

"I… I'm sorry," she said, her voice raspy and broken.

Hayden placed his fingers on her neck and felt her

pulse. "Tachycardia," he said. "She's hypovolemic."

"Do we need to take her to the hospital?" Elle asked.

"No, please," Abby begged. "I don't want to go to the hospital. Can you just fix me up Hayden?"

"That's a tall order without blood and fluids," Hayden replied. "We should get her to the hospital."

"Please, Hayden," Abby repeated her plea. "I'll do anything."

"Babe, get a blanket from the bed to cover Abby up," Hayden told Elle. "I don't need her to get hypothermic also."

Hayden thought for a few moments as Elle covered Abby's nude body with the comforter from her bed and tucked it around her body. As he considered his options, he concluded that there was only one thing that might work. One thing that he had just learned from Bilv'at and never attempted before.

"I'll try," Hayden finally told Abby. "But if this doesn't work, then you're going to the hospital before you get acidotic and die."

As he concentrated on the spell, Hayden placed his hand on Elle's arm to keep her outside the effects of the time freeze. He felt a chill run down his spine as time slowed to a standstill.

"Will this work?" Elle asked.

"I don't know," Hayden admitted. "I'm going to use a spell that I just learned, so I've never actually seen it work. These powers and spells were meant to be used by the Princess of Time. Bilv'at told me that a male has never been able to wield these powers before, and that I am only able to use them because of my status as the cognizant one. So, cross your fingers."

Hayden grasped the amulet and it shimmered with a purple hue. The room around them seemed to blur and shake. Abby's body fidgeted in response to the spell. Hayden strained as he attempted to intensify the effects.

"I think it's working," Hayden mumbled as he continued.

Elle watched as the blood that had been soaking through the makeshift bandages on Abby's arms started to disappear.

"I'm getting nauseous," Elle said as the shaking continued.

Hayden's body jerked back as he found himself unable to hold the spell any longer. The visual effects on the room stabilized and Abby opened her eyes again. Time was back to normal. Hayden removed the towels from Abby's arms.

"The cuts are healed," Elle said, surprised.

"Go check the bathwater," Hayden told her.

Elle peeked her head around the corner and looked into the bathroom. "The blood is gone from the water."

"What did you do?" Abby asked, her normal voice beginning to return.

"The spell is a localized reversal of time," Hayden replied. "Luckily, Elle found you really quick, because I was only able to hold the spell long enough to reverse several minutes."

"Thank you," Abby said.

"I'm still going to give you some fluids as a precaution," Hayden told her, then spoke to Elle. "Babe, I'm going to open a portal to our place. Can you go through it and grab my medical supply bag?"

"Yeah, of course," Elle answered.

Elle brought the bag back through the portal and Hayden dug through it to retrieve a pouch of intravenous crystalloids. He moved a floor lamp near Abby's head to hang the pouch from.

Twenty minutes later, Hayden removed the line and helped Abby up to sit on her bed. She seemed to be responding normally and was able to answer basic questions.

"Elle, can you grab some clothes for Abby and help her get dressed?" Hayden asked as he tossed the comforter back on the bed. "I'm going to send you two back to our apartment while I clean this place up. Keep an eye on Abby and call me if you need anything. I won't be too long."

After the girls walked through the newly opened portal into Hayden and Elle's apartment, Hayden focused on making Abby's apartment presentable. He swept up the broken glass from the bathroom and living room, cleaned the bathtub, and arranged any items that had been disheveled.

"So, we need to talk," Hayden said to Abby as he came through a portal into the apartment. "Judging from the condition of your place and the distinct bruising on your neck, I think you have some stuff you need to tell me."

"I'm okay," Abby replied. "It was nothing."

"She texted me a little before I got there saying that her and Jared had a really big fight," Elle chimed in. "Sorry, Abby, but I have to tell him."

"Okay, tell me the truth, Abby," Hayden insisted. "What happened?"

"Jared was mad at me," Abby said after a long sigh. "He didn't know who I was texting and he accused me of cheating on him. He got more upset and he grabbed my neck and then pushed me up against the wall. He was choking me for so long I thought I was going to pass out. Then he left and went to the bar."

"Has this happened before?" Hayden asked.

"Yes," Abby admitted. "Every time he apologizes and says it won't ever happen again. Then everything is good for a week or maybe two. He makes it seem like it's my fault and honestly for some reason I convince myself that he's right. After we got home from Thanksgiving dinner last year, he was mad that I was talking to Dan and he hit me. I think he broke one of my ribs that night, but I didn't say anything to anyone."

"You and Jared are done," Hayden said, his drawn out sigh teeming with anger.

"I can handle this," Abby insisted. "I'll talk to him and I'll leave him."

"We're past that point, Abby," Hayden replied. "You're staying here until I feel like you're okay mentally to go home, unless you'd rather spend the time in observation at the hospital. I will handle your breakup with Jared."

"Hayden…" Abby started, but was cut short as he disappeared into a portal.

ᔕ ᔕ ᔕ ᔕ ᔕ ᔕ

Abby's Apartment

The lock on the front door made the characteristic sound as

Jared turned his key. As he walked in, he saw Hayden seated on the couch.

"Oh, hey man, what's up?" Jared asked. "Is Abby here?"

"No she's out with Elle," Hayden replied. "She needed to blow off a little steam, I guess. Sounds like you two got in a fight?"

"Yeah, it was nothing," Jared said, though Hayden could see the glint of rage momentarily flash through his eyes.

"You guys fight often?" Hayden asked, trying to elicit a response.

"No, dude, this was pretty much the first time," Jared replied.

"Oh okay," Hayden said. "Except for the fact that that's bullshit. I saw the bruising on her neck from you choking her. She told me about you hitting her. You and Abby are over."

"That's not for you to decide," Jared snapped back as he walked toward Hayden.

"Is this a fight that you really want to pick?" Hayden asked.

"You think I can't take you?" Jared replied.

"No, Jared, I don't," Hayden said. "I think you're used to beating up on girls. I think you have no idea what is coming to you."

As Jared closed the gap between himself and Hayden, he cocked his arm back and threw a punch. Hayden caught the fist mid-swing and used his other hand to project a forceful gust of Air against Jared's chest, sending him flying backward against the wall.

Electricity crackled in Hayden's palm as Jared rose to his feet. The look of smug defiance disappeared from Jared's face.

"Fine," Jared relented. "I'll leave Abby alone. Let's just call this whole fight off between us. I can go and find another girlfriend."

"You seriously think that I'm going to knowingly put some other girl in harm's way by letting you walk out of here?" Hayden said.

"What are you going to do then… kill me?" Jared asked.

"I'm not going to do anything," Hayden replied.

Jared saw the reflection of purple light dancing on the wall in front of him as Hayden opened a portal directly behind him. Before he was able to look over his shoulder at the field, Hayden pushed him inside. Jared tumbled backward onto the cold concrete and Hayden stepped out of the portal over him.

"What is this?" Amaris asked as he turned to see his

father standing over a cowering Jared.

"This is a poor excuse for a man that needs to find punishment," Hayden replied. "Do what you will."

"I knew that you weren't *completely* good," Amaris said. "Maybe there's hope for you yet."

"Understand this, Amaris," Hayden replied. "It would be wise and beneficial for you to cease any desire for revenge against me or Elle. You should make an attempt at letting go and moving on. You won't win."

Amaris smirked as Hayden turned around and opened another portal back to his apartment. The last sound that Hayden heard before the portal snapped shut behind him was that of Amaris unsheathing his sword as he walked toward Jared.

ɕꝍ ɕꝍ ɕꝍ ɕꝍ ɕꝍ ɕꝍ

Hayden and Elle's Apartment

"He won't ever be bothering you again," Hayden declared as he stepped out of the portal into the bedroom.

"What did you do?" Abby asked. "Where is Jared?"

"I took care of things," Hayden said.

"That portal was purple," Abby said. "That means you

were somewhere else in time. Where did you take him?"

"Oh my God, babe," Elle said as she realized what Hayden must have done.

"Jared denied everything," Hayden said. "Then he attacked me. Then he begged for me to let him go. If I did that, then he would just end up traumatizing some other girl. A girl that I wouldn't know and wouldn't be able to save."

"You gave him to Amaris?" Elle asked. Hayden simply replied with a nod.

"Hayden!" Abby screamed. "You are not the judge, jury, and executioner. You had no right to decide this on your own. I could have dealt with it."

"Listen to yourself, Abby," Hayden replied. "He abused you, repeatedly. You have been in a good place for years now, and he undid all of that. He drove you to kill yourself. If Elle hadn't shown up when she did, you would be dead, and that would be on him. Who knows how many other girls he's done this to, who knows if any of them weren't saved in time. He got the punishment he deserved… and for the record, I didn't perform any execution."

"I can't believe you, Hayden," Abby said through her tears. "Leave me alone, take me back home. I don't want to see you or talk to you ever again."

"Sorry, Abby," Hayden replied. "I can't let you go on

like this. I can't let you live like this... and I won't let this scar you for the rest of your life. Not when you were doing so well."

Abby watched as Hayden approached her. She pushed herself back against the edge of the couch, attempting to escape. Hayden placed his hand on her head and her body fell limp.

"What are you doing, babe?" Elle asked.

"I'm erasing all her memories of Jared and her attempt at suicide," Hayden replied. "I'm not going to let her suffer for the rest of her life because she fell victim to some asshole."

"Is that..." Elle began a question, but her words faltered.

"Ethical?" Hayden finished her sentence. "Is it the right thing to do? It does more good than harm. Right now, that's the only scale I have to weigh this on. If I don't do this, she'll more than likely finish the job she started today before you found her."

"This stays between you and me then," Elle said. "I won't say a word to anyone."

ભ ભ ભ ભ ભ ભ

The Next Evening

"So, kiddo, are you gonna stay sixteen or are you going to be a baby again?" Dan asked Kiera as everyone sat in Hayden and Elle's living room. "I was never really clear on what was going to happen with all of that."

"I don't know, actually," Kiera replied. "You'd have to ask my father."

"I think that for the time being, it's best to keep her aged up," Hayden chimed in. "The threat from Amaris isn't gone completely. This is probably just a lull before retaliation. After everything has been handled, if Kiera wants me to reverse the effects of the spell, then I will."

"It's just so crazy to think about the fact that a couple days ago I was holding you in my arms," Abby said to Kiera. "Now you're here hanging out with us. You're a fully functional young woman."

"Fully functional?" Dan joked. "She's not a robot."

"You know what I mean, Dan!" Abby replied. "Like, she skipped all those years in between baby and sixteen, but she knows so many things."

"My dad transferred all that knowledge into my mind," Kiera said. "I feel like I've lived my whole life up until now, but at the same time, I'm aware that I haven't."

"Okay, so that part must be weird," Dan admitted. "What do you think, Elle?"

"I miss being able to hold my little baby girl," Elle replied. "At the same time, I don't miss changing her diapers. I think she should be able to have a full childhood if that's what she wants."

"Damn, most days I wouldn't mind being able to go back and be a kid again," Dan said.

"We can make that happen," Hayden joked as a purple light began to swirl over his open palm.

"I'm good," Dan replied. "I'm not going to put my parents through raising me again."

"You're assuming that they wouldn't just orphan you," Hayden jested.

"True, that's probably more likely," Dan said with a laugh.

"What about Amaris?" Kiera asked.

"What about him?" Hayden replied.

"He's kind of like an orphan," Kiera said. Everyone's attention moved to her. "He's never really had anyone. You're not going to kill him, right?"

"Baby girl, that's a tough question," Hayden replied. "I don't want to. If he threatens your life though... or your mother's life, then I will choose saving you."

"I just don't think that he's inherently evil," Kiera said. "We don't understand what he's going through. It has to be really hard."

"He seems to want revenge," Hayden told her. "Apparently, that includes harming all of us. I do agree that he probably thinks there are justifiable reasons, but that is misguided. The way he has gone about things is unacceptable."

"Kiera, before you two arrived, Amaris did hurt me," Elle added. "It was a very painful experience. He was about to take things in a very dark direction."

"I know," Kiera replied. "I just hope that you try to save him if you can."

"If I can," Hayden said with a nod.

"So, are we heading to dinner?" Dan interrupted, trying to change the subject to something else. "By the way, Abby, is Jared not joining us tonight?"

"Who is that?" Abby answered.

Elle shot Hayden a glace, while Dan sat with a confused look on his face.

"Hey, Dan, come help me grab something out of the car," Hayden said as he stood up. Dan followed him out to the garage.

"What is that all about?" Dan asked.

"Abby doesn't remember Jared," Hayden said.

"Obviously," Dan said. "Why not?"

"He ended up being a jackass that wasn't good for her," Hayden replied. "So the decision was made to just erase him from her memory."

"Wow, she just had you wipe him completely from her mind?" Dan asked, but then continued speaking before getting an answer. "I knew he was no good. I saw him hovering over her all intimidating-like in the restroom at your wedding reception. She swore everything was okay and that it was a one-time thing. She made me promise not to tell anyone. Anyway, I'm glad she dumped his ass. She's way too good for that jerk."

"Yeah, agreed," Hayden said, holding back the entire truth. "Just refrain from mentioning his name or anything related to him. She won't remember it."

"Done," Dan said. "He's practically erased from my mind as well."

"Cool," Hayden replied. "I meant to tell you earlier, but there's been so many things going on that I forgot. Now I just have to tell Armond. Anyway, let's go back inside, get the girls, and head to dinner."

ભ ભ ભ ભ ભ ભ

1849 AD

Ahwahnee (Yosemite Valley)

Amaris stepped out of the bright orange portal and into the lush valley. His thoughts flashed back to the moment he had first visited the area. While the story he had told Hayden about Yosemite being the first place he arrived at on Earth wasn't true, he had visited briefly before going to Orange County so that he could see the place the Alva'ci had emerged from.

He looked around and immediately noticed that the landscape was exponentially more beautiful. The vegetation seemed greener, the sky more clear, and there was a distinct absence of the traces of human activity.

"My father was using his portals to travel through time instantaneously," Amaris said to himself. "There's only one place that he could have possibly learned how to do that. I know what I need now."

As Amaris trudged through the brush of the forest, he focused his thoughts on the Alva'ci. He searched for an hour before finding the location he was looking for. A spot in the Earth's crust that was more conducive to the unique power signature of the alien creature. Amaris stood next to the face of the mountain and focused a beam of energy on the slab of stone. Once he had cut an entry, he hollowed out a room.

"Now to build the finishing touches," Amaris said to himself.

He collected a pile of smooth black stones and placed them in the center of the room. Using his powers, he melded the stone into a table. Finally, he etched the name of the Alva'ci into the stone with Fire. Amaris ripped a piece of the orange rock from the walls of the cavern and placed it on the table.

The ground beneath Amaris' feet started to rumble and the stone table in the center of the room grew hot to the touch. Steam rose from around the orange stone as new etchings appeared in the table near the one Amaris had inscribed. After several hours of patiently waiting, the activity ceased. The stone glowed faintly as Amaris picked it up.

"My very own amulet," Amaris declared as he wrapped the edges of the stone in a jet-black titanium bail and matching chain, then placed the finished product around his neck. "This will enhance my power a hundred-fold. Just a few more pieces of the puzzle to go and I'll be unstoppable."

Amaris exited the cavern and concealed the entrance with an illusionary spell. He paused for several minutes, breathing in the crisp air and listening to the sounds of a nearby waterfall. In the moment of reflection, he surmised that if he didn't possess such an overwhelming urge to avenge his mother then he would be perfectly happy to live out the rest of his days in this very spot.

"To the past," he said triumphantly while grasping his new amulet and opening a portal. As he vanished into the field, the serene landscape went back as it was. As if Amaris were never there.

Ↄↄ Ↄↄ Ↄↄ Ↄↄ Ↄↄ Ↄↄ

56,000 BC
Prehistoric Mesopotamia

Amaris approached the small village. He had read bits and pieces of the layout in Powers and Practices, so he was fairly confident that he was headed in the right direction. Bilv'at came out of her dwelling to meet him.

"The son," she said as she met Amaris halfway. "I suppose you want to know what I taught your father."

"I do," Amaris confirmed.

"Very interesting timeline," Bilv'at said as she took Amaris' hand in hers. "Would you like to know your future?"

"No, I make my own decisions and my own destiny," he replied.

"Very well," Bilv'at replied as she began walking back toward her dwelling. "You are quite the unique specimen. You share genetics with an alien creature. It is unlike your father's connection with the Alva'ci. I believe that you will accomplish much in your life. Come inside and I will teach you."

"There is one spell in particular that I need to know," Amaris said as they crossed through the entryway. He looked around the room and noted the modest accommodations for someone that he had read about being extremely powerful. He glanced at the female servant in the corner of the room who appeared to be preparing a soup in a large cauldron.

"Yes, I see your intentions," Bilv'at replied. "You ask for access to very powerful magic. I should warn you that there are certain rules in this universe that cannot be broken. Some things are inevitable."

"Is this?" Amaris asked.

"You declined when I asked if you wished to know things," Bilv'at replied coldly. "You will have to find out the answer to your question on your own."

"Whatever," Amaris said. "I have a plan and everything is going accordingly so far. I can handle any bumps in the road."

"Yes, we all have plans," Bilv'at replied as she turned to

grab a large cloth-bound book from her bedside. "Some more grand than others."

"I agree," Amaris said. "While my father is content to just live a normal life with his wife and daughter, I intend to make a name for myself. I intend to rule."

"From what I've seen in my time on this planet, being content in your family can be one of the most satisfying things in life," Bilv'at advised. "For most humans, life is short and in many cases much shorter for those that seek to wage war."

"Perhaps for regular humans," Amaris countered. "I am far from ordinary. With the things that I learn from you, my time on Earth will be anything but short. My father doesn't seem to understand that his bloodline, our family, could have complete dominance over everything."

"You profess to know your father's mind," Bilv'at replied. "Do you really? Do you think that amidst all of that power he possesses, the thoughts you describe haven't crossed his mind?"

"If they have, then he gave up on them," Amaris scowled. "Or he didn't have the fortitude to properly entertain them. He is giving up so much potential for that girl Elle. I pity his weakness for her."

"Perhaps he does not want to raise your sisters in a

world where they are hated and feared by many," Bilv'at said. "The safety of his family is much more important to him and much easier to guarantee within the status quo."

"My half-sister you mean," Amaris rebuffed. "Kiera won't be an issue for him soon. His illusion of safety for his seemingly perfect family will come to an end."

"Yes, it will soon end," Bilv'at agreed. "In a most spectacular fashion. I concur with your assessment that his false confidence in his own strength will be his downfall. All of his fantasies of keeping his family safe will vanish before his eyes."

"Shall we begin?" Amaris asked, ready to get on with his plans.

"We shall," Bilv'at said as she took Amaris' amulet in her palm and presented him with the book she had been holding. "Read this and memorize it. This will grant you the ability to travel through time instantaneously through your portals, like your father is now able to."

"Perfect," Amaris said after several minutes of reading the text repeatedly. "Now, teach me about Qiyama Sihr to help my mother."

"As you wish," Bilv'at replied. She flipped through the pages of her book for several seconds before stopping on the appropriate entry. "Learn this spell. It will do what you require. You must physically touch the person that you intend to use it on."

"Got it," Amaris stated after committing the page to memory. "What else do you have?"

"Most of these are trifling compared to what you have already learned," Bilv'at said as she flipped through the pages once again. "Here, this one will serve you. It is a spell that I taught some nearby villagers as a reward for bringing me an offering of artifacts."

"The immortality spell?" Amaris asked. "I have read about you teaching this to the villagers in what are now books of history in my time. You taught this spell to my father also?"

"Near immortality," Bilv'at corrected him. "It does not last for all time, but after so many years you won't know the difference. Also, it does not make you impervious to death if you are injured. You do have an advantage there though, possessing some of the powers of your father. It is very difficult for you to become mortally injured… and yes, I did also teach your father this spell."

"Perfect," Amaris said happily. "This should be all that I need to accomplish my goals. Thank you for your help. I must be on my way now."

"Yes, of course," Bilv'at replied as she walked Amaris to the exit. "Ila al-liqaa."

Amaris immediately vanished into a portal that pulsed with vibrant purple colors. Bilv'at returned to the interior of her dwelling and sat on the plush animal-fur rug that adorned the center of the room. Her follower walked over from the fireplace with soup bowls for each of them.

"That is not the spell you taught his father," the woman said.

"I know, my dear," Bilv'at replied. "But he doesn't need to know that."

Epilogue

October Surprise

October 30, 2024 - 11:00 p.m.

H ayden found himself restless and unable to stay asleep. He looked over at Elle, who looked content and peaceful in her slumber.

"Let's go for a walk real quick," Hayden said to himself. "Maybe that'll help me get back to sleep."

The chill of the outside air swept over Hayden's body as he opened his umbrella and stepped out on the front porch. The pitter-patter of steady raindrops on the fabric was calming. Hayden walked to the end of the street and turned right. There were no cars on the roads and all of his neighbors were shut up snugly in their homes. After a quarter mile, Hayden turned around and headed back toward his origin.

Coming back into the bedroom, Hayden stripped off his pajamas and crawled back into bed. He was careful to not rub up against Elle, as he was certain that his cold skin would wake her in a less than jovial mood. After staring at the ceiling for a few minutes, Hayden finally dozed back off to sleep.

The lightning storm inside his dream was more raucous and vicious than the fall drizzle he had encountered outside. Bolts of electric current riddled the sky and tore into the grassy field as they made landfall. The sky was dark, the only light a glimmer of city lights in the distance, visible over the precipice of a cliff's edge. The scene was familiar, the same cliff and city as Hayden had seen in another dream several months ago.

In the momentary flashes of light, Hayden made out the figure of a person standing at the edge of the cliff. He walked closer to the figure as the chorus of thunder and crackle of lightning filled the air.

As he neared the edge of the cliff, the figure became more clear in the electric flashes. Her blonde hair blew freely in the whipping winds, while she seemed to intently stare at the distant city lights below. It was the same girl that had been in his previous dream. Hayden thought about the warning she had uttered before, that not all people who seem to be friends really are. It now immediately reminded him of Amaris. His thoughts were interrupted by the girl's voice.

"Father," she said as she turned around.

Hayden stepped closer to her. The girl was just under five feet tall, with striking blue eyes that seemed to grow more intense in the near-constant pulses of lightning. He guessed that she was around twelve years old. He realized that she reminded him of Elle at a younger age. She stepped away from the edge of the cliff to within a foot of Hayden and took his hand. Even though she was soaking wet from the freezing rain, her grip was exceedingly warm.

"Father," she repeated. "I am on my way."

"On your way?" Hayden asked.

"In thirty-six weeks," the girl proclaimed.

"Elle is pregnant with you," Hayden deduced. "The disturbances in the dreamscape… the cracks of light and the black cat, was that you? I haven't had any time to figure it out and it's been bothering me."

"Yes, that was me," the girl said.

"How?" Hayden asked. "How is it even possible for you to disrupt the dreamscape? You're not even born yet."

"I will explain everything when we meet in person," the girl answered. "There isn't time right now. It takes a lot of energy for me to reach you this way and this dream is going to end soon."

"You're going to explain it to me as a baby?" Hayden asked.

"Things are going to happen," the girl replied. "We will be talking to each other soon. In the meantime, try to enjoy the relative peace in your life… while it lasts."

"What is your name?" Hayden asked as he felt the dream beginning to slip away from him.

Hayden snapped out of his dream and looked at the clock on his phone. It was seven o'clock in the morning. The dream still hung in his mind. The vivid, intricate details, the realism of the weather, so real that he could almost smell the rain still. His palm was warm, the heat from the girl's hand apparently crossing the threshold of dream and reality. The girl's last word, the answer to Hayden's final question, lingered in his consciousness like a whisper. He rose from the bed and walked to the bathroom. As Hayden returned to the bedside, Elle yawned and opened her eyes.

"Good morning, babe," Elle said as she saw Hayden looking at her.

"Hi there, my love," Hayden replied, with a sly smirk on his face.

"What's up?" Elle asked.

"You should take this," Hayden replied as he held out a pregnancy test in his hand.

"What? Why?" Elle asked confused by the sudden request.

"Let's just call it a hunch," he replied.

Elle rubbed her eyes and sighed as she convinced her body to get out of bed for the day. Hayden followed her to the bathroom and then handed her the test.

"How did you know?" Elle asked as she watched the test report a definitive positive result.

"I had a dream about her last night," Hayden said.

"Her?" Elle remarked as she giggled. "Us girls already outnumber you… and now there's going to be another one of us?"

"And that's perfectly fine with me," Hayden replied as he wrapped his arms around Elle and held her in a long embrace.

ဢ ဢ ဢ ဢ ဢ ဢ

One Week Later

Hayden walked up behind Elle, who was standing at the kitchen counter preparing breakfast. He pushed his body against hers and wrapped his arms around her.

"Good morning," she said, as she turned her head and kissed Hayden.

"Indeed it is," Hayden agreed. "That smells delicious."

"Kiera!" Elle shouted as her and Hayden sat down at the table to eat. "Breakfast is ready."

Hayden dug in and savored the momentary return to quasi-peace. He knew that the struggle wasn't over, but chose to enjoy the moments that he could. His fork scraped along the plate as he finished his meal.

"Kiera!" Hayden called out. "Your food is going to be cold."

"I'll go get her," Elle said as she stood and walked toward the hallway.

Hayden picked up the dirty dishes and began to wash them in the sink. The aroma of Elle's cooking still hung in the air, lulling Hayden into a false sense of security.

"Babe!" Elle yelled from Kiera's bedroom.

When he entered the room, Elle was standing with her arm outstretched. She grasped a note in her hand. The tears running down her cheeks and the absence of Kiera in the bedroom were clear indicators to Hayden that this wasn't good. He took the note from Elle's hand and read it.

"Mother and father, I have gone to be with Amaris.

He understands me and I love him. Please do not follow me."

The note ended with Kiera's signature. Hayden visibly seethed as he set the letter down on the nightstand. He found himself lost in thought as Elle hugged him.

"I have to go after her," Hayden said. "She's obviously being controlled by him. Kiera wouldn't do this of her own volition. It makes absolutely no sense. How did he get into her head?"

"Bring her back, please," Elle agreed. "Bring our daughter back."

☙ ☙ ☙ ☙ ☙ ☙

Dan sat on the couch at Abby's apartment, while she flipped through the channels on the television with no particular program in mind.

"So, do you remember last Thanksgiving?" Dan asked, trying to heed Hayden's warning about not bringing up Jared. However, he still wanted to know what she remembered.

"Yeah, of course," Abby replied. "It was a really good meal. Hayden's parents were there and Clark and Sam came out. How could I forget?"

"Right," Dan agreed, snorting that she made no mention of him asking her out a week prior to

Thanksgiving. "I was thinking maybe we could all do something together again this year. It was really nice having everyone back around."

"Yeah, hopefully everyone can visit again," Abby agreed. "It was fun."

"This time we can even have Thanksgiving up at Hayden and Elle's house in Camarillo," Dan said. "So much more room than their apartment, plus that heated pool and the jacuzzi."

"Thank you for hanging out with me these past few days," Abby said. "I've had a lot of fun, even if we've just been watching movies and eating tons of fast food."

"Of course. I'm glad to be here," Dan replied. "I really like hanging out with you. I really like being around you, Abby."

"Careful, it almost sounds like you have a crush on me," Abby joked as she prodded Dan's arm.

"Right. You wouldn't want that, huh?" Dan said, his tone more defeated than joking.

"I ummm..." Abby stammered, noticing that Dan had suddenly become serious.

"Would that be such a bad thing, if I had a crush on you?" Dan asked. In his own mind it was almost a rhetorical question, given how Abby had responded last year.

"Dan, it would be a bad thing for you," Abby's tone switched to match Dan's seriousness. "I'm not anyone that you want to be with. It's not that I don't like you or that I couldn't see us as more than friends, but I don't want you to have to suffer through a relationship with me. I'm not girlfriend material. I put on a good front, but I'm not some magnificent prize of a human being."

"That's nonsense," Dan retorted. "Sure, maybe you have issues. I have issues too. We all do. But you're an amazing person. You're one of my favorite people in the world. You're smart, empathetic, driven, and fun. Even with how awesome you are, you're still humble and compassionate. You don't need to be alone. You need someone that understands you and will support you no matter what."

"Okay, wow, you've really thought this through," Abby said, her voice reflecting the fact that she wasn't expecting Dan's answer. "I just don't want to hurt you, Dan."

"Let me worry about me," Dan replied. "I know that I joke around a lot, but I also know that I have the ability to have a mature relationship… and that if things aren't working out, I possess the capacity to end things amicably before they spiral out of control and people get hurt."

"I just… I don't know," Abby said. "Let me think

about it. You know, it's not that I don't want a relationship. I would love to… to get married, have kids, have someone to share everything with. I'm just afraid that if you see the side of me that I keep hidden, that you'll run."

"Okay, think about it," Dan replied. "Take your time. I can wait until you decide. In the meantime, I'll still be here to hang out every day if you want. Just… now you know. I love you as a friend, Abby. If you decide that we have to remain friends, then I can deal with that. I just think that I might love you as more than a friend also. I think that maybe we could be happy together."

"Please, do continue to come hang out," Abby said. "It's been great having you around the past few days. I promise that I will think about it. It might take a little while. I'm not saying that I'll have an answer for you tomorrow or anything. But I will think about it and I will give you an answer. Just be patient with me."

"You got it," Dan replied. "So, what do you want for dinner tonight?"

"I was hoping that maybe we could go out to Quesada's," Abby said. "Get out of the apartment and get some fresh air."

"Sounds good to me," Dan said. "I'll grab my keys."

______

Appendix I

The Ancient Powers

The several powers, or magical abilities, are first seen in use in 54,000 BC (see Agents of Fate: Chapter Three). At that point in time, they became dormant in humans due to a spell performed by Abbas. Their traces were passed on, although they were undetectable to their bearers and the powers unusable.

In 2022, a prophecy came true when Hayden de Vere turned out to be the foretold cognizant one. The appearance of the cognizant one was prophesied by Abbas in a vision approximately two years after the Alva'ci came to Earth. As the bearers of the dormant powers began to die off in 2022, the powers began to manifest once again in their real forms.

Little information is known about the origination of the magical abilities and how or when humans acquired them. It is rumored that there is a book of lore, written by Abbas when he was close to his death, that conveys the secrets that humans used to acquire their magical abilities. Whether or not this book exists is known only to the descendants of Abbas.

The Powers and Their Symbols:

Elemental Powers:

Water ماء   Fire نار

Earth أرض   Air جو

Sub-Elemental Powers:

Light ضوء   Energy طاقة

Shadow ظل   Electricity برق

Non-Elemental Powers:

Ane'illuminus / Thought خاطِر

The Seven Spells نوبات

The Seven Spells:

Abarus - Otherworldly Warriors

Tithethus - The Bindings

Emiratus - Power Amplification

Prophesch'naya Con'di Ashante - Shroud of Darkness

Chantiatus - Protective Forcefields

Youlvasius - Lucky Strikes

Amal Esta Preavius - Energy Portals

The Eighth Spell:

Nelitus Absoritum Malitus - Alva'ci Banishment

The Forbidden Spell:

E'it ad'a Layadänte

Several additional spells have been revealed or made since the emergence of the agents of fate. The Alva'ci taught Hayden de Vere their method of time travel, which involved a spell developed by its species. Hayden has shown himself capable of altering or developing new spells after the creation and development of his amulet.

Amaris casts a spell that he learned from Powers and Practices during a moment of desperation. This spell redefined everything for Hayden as he was facing defeat, and in a twist of fate, made it possible for him to triumph.

Appendix II

The Prophecies

Abbas recorded several prophecies and visions shortly before he passed away. The following selections are relevant to this entry in The Agents of Fate Series.

The Abassilon Prophecy

53993 BC

At once, you awake and find yourself in a new world,
a new beginning.
The scars of time, though stinging at times,
are dulled from passing years.
Memories of nights that shall never be forgotten
flash through your mind from time to time,
to remind you of all that was had, of all that was lost.

You walk upon the sands,
on the beach of this new land..
journeying to something yet unknown.
You see a girl, standing alone by the water's edge.
Her golden hair flowing in the breeze, her voice fair and sweet.
Her eyes, while calm and inviting,
also piercing and hiding much behind them.

As you walk nearer, flashes of destiny
race through your mind like precognitive deja vu.
What path is coming to emerge?
You can feel it in your bones,
if you approach her, a piece of your life will be hers.

They've called you many things...
they focused on the darkness that swirled around you.
And though they were mistaken,
as magnificence can oft be mistook for darkness,
they never understood.
But as you look onward toward the girl,
you can see the light from within her.

...and the light shall mingle with the darkness, and together
they shall shine with a brilliance both dazzling and fearsome.

———

She turns to see you and you look into her eyes.
Suddenly you understand,
and together you walk toward the city.

~~E'it ad'a layadänte~~
We shall share this path

The Prophecy of Hindrant Salvas
53980 BC

Pacing the grounds, hollow footsteps echo into oblivion.
Turning round, facing the reality of duplicity.

Into the waters, knee-deep. The rip current drawing you in.
The seduction that you both play on each other
is providential.

What can you have?
Is it greater than anything you've been given?
What remains to be seen,
shall determine the course of revisionist history.

Turning a corner into the halls of life yet written.
Through the doorway and into an empty room.

We have come to dance here,

a dance careful and indifferent.

Setting the night ablaze with aberrant passions.

The world outside these windows, vast and insignificant.

Who you are at dusk is not the you of dawn.

Reaching a precipice, fraught with lasting decisions.

How do you get what you want,

when what you want is everything?

Appendix III

The Books of Lore

Abbas wrote several books that were passed down to the firstborn of each generation of his family. These books contained the lore concerning the Agents of Fate. The current keeper of the books of lore is Armond el-Hashem. Among the known volumes are:

The Conqueror الفاتح

An account of the arrival of the Alva'ci on Earth. This book contains first-hand accounts from Abbas, Ahjiamed, Koshili, and dozens of other members of their village. Also included are charts and drawings depicting the creature, a sky chart detailing where the Alva'ci entered the atmosphere, and a description of the orange rock that the creature's armor consisted of.

Prophecies and Visions نبوءات ورؤى

After the victory obtained over the Alva'ci in 54,000 BC, Abbas began to have visions pertaining to the nature of the Agents of Fate and future events that concerned those that held the remnants of power. This book of lore is a collection of the visions and prophecies that Abbas made until his death at the age of 387. One of the most prominent prophecies included was The Parisifian Prophecy. This prophecy foretold the eventual appearance of the Cognizant One, an Agent of Fate that was unique in their abilities and would come at a time in history when the Alva'ci may possess the ability to rise again.

Powers and Practices القدرات والمهارات
(aka Abilities and Skills)

Written very late in the life of Abbas, this book of lore's existence is only rumored. It is said that this book includes detailed explanations of how humans first acquired magical abilities. Details of each magical power and its uses are included, ranging from the simplest forms to advanced techniques that came with aptitude and skill. The book includes a detailed account of the power of Ane'illuminus and the achievements made by those that mastered the power within their lifetimes. A section of the lore includes an account of how Abbas and a handful of others were able to artificially extend their lives to seemingly unnatural ages through the masterful use of the magical powers. Finally, Abbas included warnings concerning the use of The Forbidden Spell (which is mentioned in The Abassilon Prophecy, but with the words crossed out to prevent its use). The warnings also included several accounts of various magic users that attempted the spell only to meet their immediate deaths.

Appendix IV

Glossary

A'ltal Bilv'at – translates to "the power of Bilv'at." A term used by Abbas and other villagers to describe a spell taught to their ancestors by the entity Bilv'at.

Alva'ci – a species of alien lifeform. Origin unknown. The term is also used to identify the singular creature that arrived on planet Earth in 54,000 BC (The Alva'ci).

Bilv'at – an entity that resides on Earth in the form of a human woman. Rumored to be a Principality, but actual origin and nature unknown. Active in historical records between 56,000 - 54,000 BC, but said to have existed before that time period as well.

Breaker Books – a bookstore located in Manhattan's Upper West Side neighborhood. The shop is owned by the brothers Armond and Ahsan el-Hashem.

About the Author

Tony Contratto writes books, this much we know. In his free time, he is also a small business owner and nonprofit director. Tony's philosophy is that the most gripping and immersive tales happen in our imagination. In the spirit of that ideology, Tony spent several years formulating the story of his first novel within his head, before ever putting the proverbial pen to paper. Originally from Southern California, Tony now resides in Lake Havasu City, Arizona. Visit Tony at his website and follow him on social media at contrattos.net

Coming Soon

**Faced with the impossible, could you find
your way back to the ones you love?**

On the precipice of losing everything he holds dear, Hayden de Vere endures his most challenging tribulation in a desperate attempt to make things right in the world. The events of a discarded past bring haunting clarity to the present. Tragedy and heartache seemingly surround every member of the inner circle. Ancient forces awaken and throw the entire future into question.

Join Hayden, Elle, Abby, and Dan as
The Agents of Fate Series
continues with the **fourth** installment:

Descendants of Wrath

*"We have come to dance here, a dance careful and indifferent.
Setting the night ablaze with aberrant passions."*

එ එ එ එ එ එ

Sign up for the Insider Email Newsletter and receive
a FREE exclusive copy of the prequel story
AOF: The Distant Shadow
agentsoffate.com

More To Read

The Agents of Fate Series

begins with

Agents of Fate

*"Really enjoyed! Right from the beginning the story drew me in.
After that, every chapter ended with me not wanting to put it down."*

കു കു കു കു കു കു

Set fifteen years before Book One,
make sure to read the prequel story

The Distant Shadow

കു കു കു കു കു കു

Thank you for reading!

If you enjoyed this book, please take a moment to
add a review on Amazon and/or Goodreads.

www.ingramcontent.com/pod-product-compliance
Lightning Source LLC
Chambersburg PA
CBHW032032310726
48972CB00002B/645